喚醒你的英文語感！

Get a Feel for English !

4週商英致勝企畫

BIZ
上班族週末充電課
TELEPHONE
ENGLISH

電話英文

作者◎申藝娜　審閱◎Quentin Brand

Would you like me to
take a message?

週休二日快速充電，躋身全球化職場即戰力！

　　我在台灣擔任英語講師二十多年，許多學生和客戶告訴我，他們在進入職場後才意識到，無論規模大小，亦無關外商企業或高科技貿易公司，良好的英語能力對本身的職務都扮演著舉足輕重的關鍵，出色的英語能力能帶來相對大的競爭優勢是無庸置疑的，然而卻都爲時已晚——因爲開始工作之後，才發現根本沒有完整的時間進修英語。早知道當初在學校裡上英文課時，就應該更認眞學習云云。

　　和爲了通過考試而研讀英語者不同，與其鑽研文法，上班族所需要的是立即有用的"Real English"。事實上，上班族每天從事的工作大多是雷同的。例如，打電話給同事、廠商或顧客詢問或確認事項；出席會議討論和解決問題；發表簡報以展示新產品或報告執行成果等。而在這些情境之下，使用的語言範圍非常小，其實相當易於學習與應用。

　　本書從最簡單和最常見的詞組開始，囊括最常見的語句、對話，旨在幫助讀者輕鬆完成接聽、撥打、轉接等任務，除了日常實務之外，更納入了有助維繫商務情誼和處理緊急狀況的各種實用句。另外，附加的 CD 則收錄了全書所有例句，是培養聽力的重要工具——別忘了，聽力也是完美應對英語電話的一項基本技能，聽力和口說能力的建構是相輔相成的。

　　總而言之，本系列對於那些尚未學習商務英語的人而言，是一個很好的入門，而對那些已經在工作中使用英語但需要一些改進的人來說，則是一個簡潔扼要的複習。我眞誠地推薦它。

Quentin Brand

工作太忙，根本沒有時間可以好好加強英語嗎？

　　如果你是任職於跨國企業，或是需要經常與國外的生意夥伴在電話線上溝通的上班族，那麼英語應該帶給你相當大的壓力吧？你是否也曾下定決心：「這次一定要把英語學好」、「下個月開始，下班後去上英語補習班」……但是，在忙碌的工作與生活中很難實踐，對吧？有鑑於此，我特別為了這樣的你，撰寫了這本書——只要在週末分別投資兩個小時，就能不吃力地學好實用的商務英語。

　　本書就是為了那些工作上需要用英語通電話，但是一拿起話筒就緊張到說不出話的上班族所設計的。英語會話已經夠難了，在電話線上用英語談論公事更是會讓人冒出冷汗；如果是面對面說話，至少可以觀察對方的眼神、表情和手勢來掌握氣氛，然而這在電話中是做不到的。就算是用我們的母語來講電話有時都很難理解對方的反應，更何況是用英語通話！

　　各位，現在可以將拿起話筒前的緊張通通拋開了。本書將各種商務電話用語分成 16 課，每一課皆列舉了最常說和最常聽到的 10 種說法，帶領讀者熟悉至少 160 種核心表達方式。另外，並提供相關例句與替換用法。藉由本書，相信不僅能加強英語實力，更有助於提升自信心——外語學習中相當重要的一環。

　　無論讀者是為了什麼目的學英語，都請務必記得：英語必須透過持續不斷的學習才會進步，因此請不要中途放棄，持續一個月看看吧。星期六與星期日各兩小時的英語充電課，將會大大減輕平日的工作壓力。好，那就從本週末開始吧！

申藝娜

讓溝通討論更有效率的
商務電話英語週末特訓

〉〉**網羅所有英語電話之通關表達句！**

– 160 個實用句型
囊括五百多組從基本的撥‧轉‧接電話開始，到日常職務中最常使用的語句、對話，以及錄製語音訊息與應對緊急狀況時所須的各種說法。

– 4 週看見成效
為使平常忙到幾乎無暇好好休息的上班族能在短時間內掌握上百種商務電話必備表達方式，本書將內容規劃成四週課程，讀者僅須撥出星期六和星期日各兩個小時，集中時間、精力研讀各兩堂課必有所進步。

– 融入人物角色提升學習樂趣
為幫助記憶並增添臨場感，本書特別設計插畫角色貫穿全場，包含初入國際職場、對商務英語略顯生疏的菜鳥職員，以及名為 Kate 的女老師，讓容易流於單調的英語學習過程變得較為有趣，各位讀者不妨以像是在上家教課一般，和書中角色一起練習。

〉〉本書附贈之 CD 收錄全書嚴選句型、例句和全篇對話內容，檔案格式為 MP3 檔。由外師配音專業錄製，時間約 95 分鐘，容量約 131 MB。

哎呦～
我很有空耶～

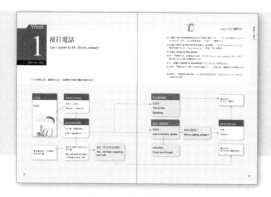

"上課前"
流程圖與重點提示

將該課程中所學到的內容一目了然地整理成流程圖，再搭配 Kate 老師傳授的重點詞彙，讓學習變得更為順暢。

"這個一定要注意"
電話英語通關句 TOP 10

介紹各情況下一定會使用到的十大語句以及延伸例句或對話，並包括淺顯易懂的說明、替換用法，以及實用的商務 TIPS。

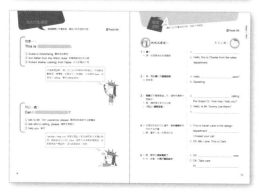

"檢視學過的表達方式"
核心句型與隨堂測驗

在每堂課之後練習主要句型與其活用法，然後透過簡短的「隨堂測驗」來驗收前面已經學過的內容。答案在每個單元最後一頁的最下方（例如 p.21）。

"確實跟讀成效佳"
複習時間

本單元對話 C. 之錄音共有兩遍，第一遍的每句之間特別保留了較長的間隔，以便讀者於空檔做跟讀練習；練習完之後，會再播放一次正常語速的版本幫助理解。

4 週英語週末特訓 *Plan*

你的電話英語實力
我瞭若指掌！
嘆呵呵呵～～～

星期日

為了早日變身為商務電話的英語達人，
外商菜鳥都用這本書來緊急充電！

Who is he?

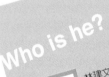

林建文（英文名字 Kevin）/
跨國企業職場新鮮人。個
性善良又誠實，只是英語
實力有夠菜。主要的工作
內容為接聽電話與協助前
輩，每次接到外國人打來
的電話都用虛弱顫抖的聲
音回答，最常聽到對方說
的話是 "Are you OK?"。
擺脫「菜英文」，不能再
拖下去了！

Who is she?

Kate Kim / 有著女神外貌
的才女兼吃貨。身為華僑
第三代的她被紐約的分公
司派到台灣，成為那些因
英語而苦惱的「英痴」們
的家教名師，最喜歡讓人
在高級餐廳請吃飯，受過
她指點的許多商務人士都
在國際舞台上蛻變成英語
高手。

Week 1

基本篇

Week

1

接打電話

Can I speak to Mr. Stone, please?

>> 正式開始之前，請跟著 Kevin 一起練習用英語打電話的基本說法。

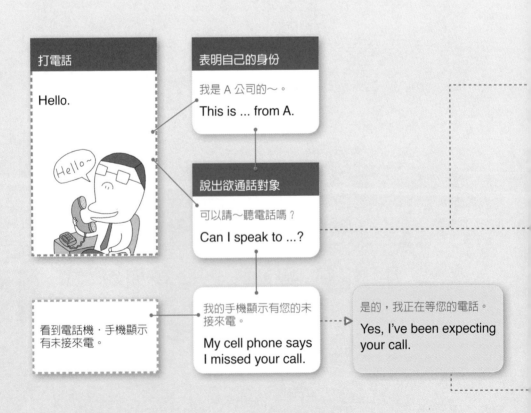

Kate 老師的重點提示

◆ 打電話 **call somebody** 因為我們是講打電話「給」～，所以很容易說成call "to" somebody。記住，call 後面直接接上人名就好，不需要加 to。

◆ 接電話 **pick up the phone** 直譯為「拿起電話」，也可用 answer 取代 pick up。電話鈴響時可以說 "I'll get the phone."，意指「我來接電話」。

◆ 掛電話 **hang up the phone**

◆ 喂？ **Hello?** 撥、接電話皆可使用。也可用 (This is) John speaking. 取代，很多人會用自己的名字當作接電話時的招呼。

◆ 和～講電話 **speak to somebody** 也可以用 talk 來替換 speak。

◆ 我是～ **This is ＋ 人名** 一般對話時會說 I'm ...，但是注意，講電話的時候要說 This is ...。

◆ 謝謝您～ **Thank you for ...** for 後接名詞或動名詞，例如 Thank you for calling.。（感謝您的來電。）

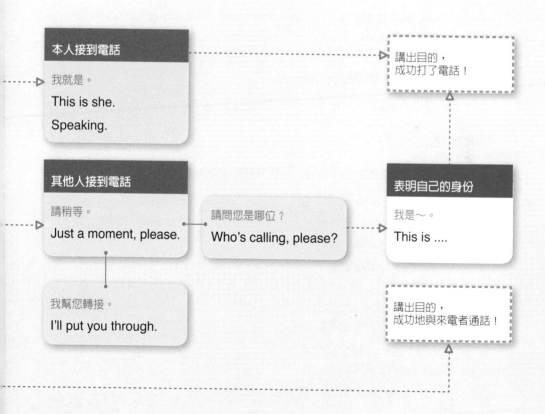

電話英語通關句 TOP 10

聽到電話那方傳來 "Hello" 的聲音就會心跳加快嗎？好，從現在起不要再害怕了，從最基礎開始練習吧。

來～相信我
想想你已經
學過的內容～

他講英文……
我該怎麼辦～

Hello

Hello?

喂？

和中文一樣，Hello? 接．打電話時皆可使用。打電話的人不要只跟接電話的人說 Hello 之後就等著對方發言，要先自我介紹或說明自己來電所找對象。

> A Hello? Is Ms. Kelly Church there? This is Jay Lee calling from Taipei.
> 喂，請問凱莉秋吉小姐在嗎？我是台北的李傑一。
>
> B Just a minute, please.
> 請稍等。

Can I speak to Mr. Stone, please?

可以請史東先生聽電話嗎？

要表明來電所找對象，就這麼說。中文有「～在嗎？」、「～現在方便講電話嗎？」等各種表達方式，英文也是，比如下列例句。

· Is Mr. Stone there?
  史東先生在嗎？

· May I speak to Mr. Stone, please?
  可以請史東先生聽電話嗎？

· Could I talk to Mr. Stone?
  可以請史東先生聽電話嗎？

· I'd like to speak to Mr. Stone, please.
  我找史東先生。

Speaking.

我就是。

接到找自己的電話時，這是最常見也最道地的回應說法。要表明「我就是」時，電話上不用 I'm ...，而應該說 This is ...。注意，This is me. 是錯誤用法！

· **This is she.**
  我就是。

· **This is David.**
  我（就）是大衛。

Who's calling, please?

請問您是哪位？

本句是在詢問來電者是誰，特別是當接到打給別人的電話時。若在前面加上 May I ask ... 聽起來更謙遜。注意，如果只問 Who is this? 的話聽起來不是很有禮貌。

· **Who am I talking to?**
  請問您哪位？

· **May I ask who's calling, please?**
  不好意思，請問您是？

This is Keith calling from Dr. Hunt's office.

我是杭特博士辦公室的凱斯。

我是「從～打電話來」就是 calling from ...。注意，此處一樣不用 I'm ...。

A Hello?
  喂？

B Hi, this is Gina Austin calling from IBN. Is Mr. Lin there?
  您好，我是 IBN 的吉娜奧斯汀。林先生在嗎？

A Speaking.
  我就是。

Thank you for calling Wade Industries.

感謝您來電偉德企業。

接聽公務電話的第一句話就這麼說，既正式也很自然。

· Thank you for calling Wade Industries. My name is Grey. How may I help you?
  感謝您來電偉德企業，我叫格雷。請問您需要什麼協助？

Do you have a minute (to talk)?

請問您方便講電話嗎？

在繁忙的上班時間裡打電話給他人，先說這句話是一種禮貌，而下面是幾種可用來替換的說法。

· Is this a bad time for you?
  您現在不方便嗎？

· Did I catch you at a bad time?
  您現在忙嗎？

· Did I wake you up?
  我有沒有吵醒您？

My cell phone says I missed your call.

我的手機顯示有您的未接來電。

發現有未接來電，回電話給對方時可以這麼說。

· Did you call me?
  你有打電話給我嗎？

· I got your message. I'm returning your call.
  我收到您的訊息所以回電。

· Thanks for your text message. So, what's up?
  謝謝你的簡訊。什麼事？

09 I have to go.

我得掛電話了。

正在忙或是需要去處理別的事情時可派上用場。不過，如果不是在講電話而是和人見面
然後結束工作時，這句話就變成「我要走了」的意思。

· I've got to go now. Goodbye.
  我現在得掛電話了，再見。

· I have to run.
  我要掛了。

· Hey, I've got to go. Can I call you back?
  嘿，抱歉我得掛了。可以待會兒回電給你嗎？

· I'll call you later.
  我再打電話給你。

· I have a call on the other line.
  我有另外一通電話要接。

10 Excuse me?

你說什麼？

本句在電話和日常對話上皆可應用。特別是有時講電話收訊不良而聽不清楚對方說什麼
時，這句話就很有用。

· I'm sorry. What did you say?
  不好意思，您說什麼？

· Say again? (= Come again?)
  什麼？（較不正式的說法，不適宜於談論公事時使用。）

· What?
  什麼？（跟對方很熟時）

彼此很熟的時候……

🎵 Track 03

朋友和家人來電時就不需要像在工作時那樣正式。下面是幾種口語上常用的表達方式。

· How are you? >> Hey, what's up? 嘿，怎麼樣？
· Long time no see! >> Long time no talk! 好久沒聊了！
· How are you doing? >> What's up, dude? 老兄，怎麼樣？（限於男性間）
· Hello, this is ... >> Hey, it's me. 嘿，是我啦。（光聽聲音就知道是誰的關係）

請確實開口反覆練習，讓自己熟悉這些句型。　　　　🔵**Track 04**

我是～。

This is _____.

① Susie in Advertising　廣告部的蘇希
② Ann Miller from the Hilton Hotel　希爾頓飯店的安米勒
③ Robert Walker (calling) from Taipei　台北的羅伯沃克

> 打商務電話時，報上自己名字的時候同時說出工作地點或
> 職稱是一種禮貌。若要表示工作地點，介系詞用 from；或
> 是加上 calling，變成 calling from。

可以～嗎？

Can I _____?

① talk to Mr. Tim Lawrence, please　請提姆勞倫斯先生聽電話
② ask who's calling, please　請問您是哪位
③ help you　幫您

> Can/May I help you? 其實在電話上是在詢問對方來電的原
> 因，最前面也可以加上 How。當對方未表明來電原因，或
> 是接到客戶電話時，這句話就能派上用場。

隨堂測驗 A

請依 CD 所播放的內容，完成下列對話。

🔊 **Track 05**

試試這樣說～

牛刀小試！

1 A: 喂？
B: 喂，我是業務部的查爾斯。

A: _____
B: Hello, this is Charles from the sales department.

2 A: 喂。可以請珍恩聽電話嗎？
B: 我就是。

A: Hello. _____ Jane?
B: Speaking.

3 A: 感謝您來電葛雷普公司，請問您需要什麼幫助？
B: 喂，請問湯米李先生在嗎？
A: （可以）請問您是？

A: _____ calling the Grape Co. How may I help you?
B: Hello. Is Mr. Tommy Lee there?
A: _____

4 A: 我是設計部的莎拉蓮恩，我手機顯示有您的未接來電。
B: 噢，蓮恩小姐，我是克拉克。

A: This is Sarah Lane in the design department. _____ I missed your call.
B: Oh, Ms. Lane. This is Clark.

5 A: 噢，我現在得掛電話了。
B: 好，保重，我再打電話給你。

A: Oh, _____ now.
B: OK. Take care.
I'll _____.

19

隨堂測驗 **B** 請聽 CD 完成下列三組不同情境的對話。

🔊**Track 06**

1 請試著打電話給蘋果企業的貝爾先生。

A: 感謝您來電蘋果企業，我是珍恩布朗。請問您需要什麼協助？

B: **我是**林建文。**請問貝爾先生在嗎？**

A: 在，請稍等。

B: **謝謝。**

A: Thank you for calling Apple Corporation. This is Jane Brown. How can I help you?

B: _____ Kevin Lin. _____

A: Yes. Just a minute, please.

B: _____

🔊**Track 07**

2 手機顯示艾拉打來的未接來電，請試著回電看看。

A: 艾拉，我是建文。

B: 嘿，建文，什麼事？

A: **我手機有妳的未接來電。**

B: 噢，對，但是我現在得掛電話。可以待會兒回電給你嗎？

A: **沒問題。**

B: OK，掰。

A: Ella, this is Kevin.

B: Hey, Kevin. What's up?

A: _____

B: Oh, yes. But I've got to go now. Can I call you back?

A: _____

B: OK. Bye.

⊙Track 08

3 請試著打電話問候吉姆派金斯先生，記得要先問對方是否方便接聽。

A: 喂？

B: 喂。**請問吉姆派金斯先生在嗎？**

A: 我就是。請問您是哪位？

B: 我是布蘭蒂克勞佛。**您現在會不會不方便？**

A: 不會，我現在可以講電話。你最近怎麼樣？

B: 我最近在忙一個新案子。

A: Hello?

B: Hello. _____

A: This is he. May I ask who's calling, please?

B: This is Brandy Crawford. _____

A: No, I can talk now. How have you been?

B: I've been busy with a new project.

Answers

轉接電話

I'll put you through.

〉〉請跟著 Kevin 一起練習用英語轉接電話的基本說法。

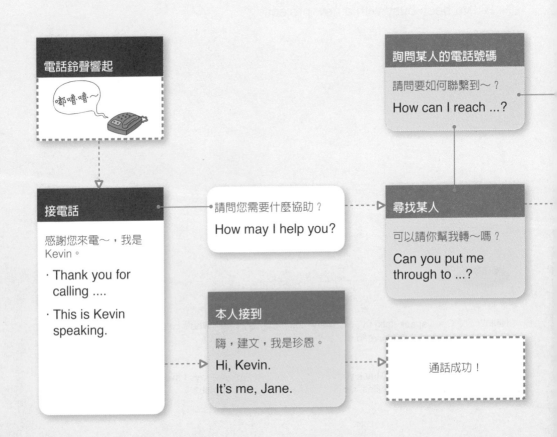

電話鈴聲響起

嘟嚕嚕～

接電話

感謝您來電～，我是 Kevin。

· Thank you for calling ....

· This is Kevin speaking.

詢問某人的電話號碼

請問要如何聯繫到～？

How can I reach ...?

請問您需要什麼協助？

How may I help you?

尋找某人

可以請你幫我轉～嗎？

Can you put me through to ...?

本人接到

嗨，建文，我是珍恩。

Hi, Kevin.

It's me, Jane.

通話成功！

Kate 老師的重點提示

◆ （請）稍等 **hang on / hold on** 兩者皆為「請等一下」之意。

◆ 我幫您轉接 **I'll put you through.** put through 指「轉接電話」。

◆ 請幫我轉～ **Can you put me through to ...?** 也可以說 Can I speak to ...?

◆ 請問要怎樣可以聯繫上～？ **How can I reach ...?** 這個句子帶有 請對方轉接給某人，或是詢問某人電話號碼的語感。reach 指「與～ 用電話聯絡」。

◆ 不掛斷請對方等 **put somebody on hold** 即讓來電者等待之意。

◆ 分機號碼 **extension number** 通常會省略只說 extension。

◆ 不能接電話 **not available** 原本是「沒有而無法使用」的意思，也 可用來形容「不在座位上或無法接聽電話」。

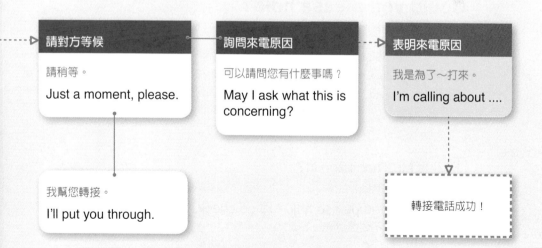

詢問分機號碼

請問～的分機幾號？

What's ...'s extension?

請對方等候

請稍等。

Just a moment, please.

詢問來電原因

可以請問您有什麼事嗎？

May I ask what this is concerning?

表明來電原因

我是為了～打來。

I'm calling about ....

我幫您轉接。

I'll put you through.

轉接電話成功！

電話英語通關句 TOP 10

不管怎麼樣，終於接起電話，但卻不是找自己的話呢？這時也不要緊張，先說「請稍等」，然後轉接給對方找的人就好了。

妳現在在哪？ 在你後面！

🔊 **Track 09**

Just a minute, please.

請稍候。

此即轉接電話之前請對方稍等時最常使用的一句話。這裡的 a minute 不是一分鐘，而是與 moment 一樣，是「片刻」的意思，因此也有很多人會說 Just a moment, please.。除此之外，下列例句也都很實用。

· **Just a second.**
請稍候。

· **Hold on just a moment.**
請稍等，不要掛斷。

· **Hang on a sec. / Just a sec.**
等一下。（與對方很熟時）

Could you please hold?

可以請您不要掛斷稍等一下嗎？

與 Just a minute, please. 相較，這句話是請對方稍微等久一點的意思，比方說 Can you hold while I go look for him, please?（請稍等，我去找他。）如果需要讓對方等更久，就可以說 I'm going to have to put you on hold.。我想大家都有過拿著電話邊聽音樂或公司廣告邊等的經驗。

A **Is Mr. Thompson in?**
請問湯普森先生在嗎？

B **Could you please hold? I'll go check.**
可以請您不要掛稍等一下嗎？我去看看。

24

I'll put you through.

我幫您轉接。

幫忙轉接電話時通常都會這麼說，也常聽到 I'll connect you. 或 I'll transfer you. 等。

A　Is Harry Butterfield there?
　　請問哈利巴特菲爾德在嗎？

B　Yes, just a moment, please, and I'll put you through.
　　在，請稍等，我幫您轉接。

Can you put me through to Mr. Harris?

可以請你幫我轉哈利斯先生嗎？

此則打電話的人請對方轉接時的說法，put me through 後面接 "to + 人名"。

· I'd like to speak to the person who's in charge of accounting.
　我想跟會計部負責人說話。

· I'm trying to reach Mr. Harris in the editorial department.
　我想找編輯部的哈利斯先生。

Is Ms. Fielder available?

請問費爾德小姐方便講電話嗎？

這是在問想找的人現在是否方便接電話，也就是請對方轉接的意思。available 是一個很好用的形容詞，原指「可以使用」，在電話上則是「現在可以通話」的意思。

A　K&G Trading Company. This is Tom Jones. How may I help you?
　　K&G 貿易公司，我是湯姆瓊斯。請問您需要什麼協助？

B　Is Ms. Fielder available?
　　請問費爾德小姐方便講電話嗎？

A　Just a moment, please.
　　請稍候。

What's his extension?

請問他的分機幾號?

通常在有使用代表號的公司裡,每個職員都會有自己的分機號碼,而「分機號碼」的英文就是 extension number,或者更常只說 extension。請對方轉接分機 123 即 Could I have extension 123, please?

A I'm trying to reach Mr. Kay. What's his extension, please?
我想找凱伊先生。請問他的分機幾號?

B Oh, it's 121.
噢,是 121。

A Thank you.
謝謝。

Who are you calling?

請問您找誰?

這個問法雖然聽起來很直接,但是不算失禮,不過也可以用 Who would you like to speak to? 替換。回答就說 Mr. Brown, please. 或 I'd like to talk to Mr. Brown.(請幫我接布朗先生)。

· Who are you trying to reach?
請問您想找哪位?

· What department are you calling?
請問您找哪個部門?

How can I reach Mr. Baker?

請問要如何聯繫到貝克先生?

此處 reach 指「與~通電話」。本句可以是請對方轉接貝克先生,也可以是詢問哪一個號碼可以聯繫到他。我們常會聽到自動電話答錄機裡有 You've reached the Baker residence. 這樣的錄音,意思就是「這裡是貝克家」。

A How can I reach Ms. Chen in the finance department?
請問要如何聯繫到財務部的陳小姐?

B Just a moment, please. I'll transfer your call.
請稍候,我為您轉接。

I'll give you his extension in case you get disconnected.

為了避免待會兒電話斷線，我給您他的分機。

有時候幫忙轉接電話時會不小心斷線，因此建議像這樣預先告知通話對象的分機號碼。
電話被斷線就是 get disconnected。

A　If you get disconnected, you can reach him at extension 554.
如果電話斷線了，你可以打分機 554 找他。

B　OK, thanks.
好，謝謝。

May I ask what this is concerning?

可以請問您有什麼事嗎？

如果接到找上司的電話，而上司又不在的話，可以先問對方有什麼事，而這是較為正式
的說法。回答就用 I'm calling about ... 此句型，例如 I'm calling about my meeting with Mr.
Ryder tomorrow.（我是為了明天跟萊德先生的會議打來）。

- What is this call regarding?
  請問您打來有什麼事？

- What are you calling about?
  請問您打來有什麼事？

各種職稱名
雖然職稱會隨著公司規模或組織型態而稍有不同，但是一般來說如下：

執行長 CEO (Chief Executive Officer)	董事長 chairman
總裁 president	副總裁 vice president
董事總經理 managing director	資深董事總經理 senior managing director
總經理 general manager	副總經理 deputy general manager
經理 manager / section chief	副理 assistant manager
監事 / 主管 supervisor	職員 clerk

核心句型練習

請確實開口反覆練習，讓自己熟悉這些句型。 **Track 10**

可以請你幫我轉～嗎？

Can you put me through to ⬤⬤⬤⬤⬤⬤⬤⬤⬤ **?**

① Mr. Smith in the sales department　業務部的史密斯先生
② the customer service center　客服中心
③ the R&D department　研發部門

> 「客服中心」這個詞會隨著公司與狀況的不同而略有差異，一般而言都是 customer service center，或是省略 center 直接說 customer service 也可以。

請問要如何聯繫到～？

How can I reach ⬤⬤⬤⬤⬤⬤⬤ **?**

① Mr. Harris　哈利斯先生
② the after-sales department　售後服務部
③ the technical support center　技術支援部

> 注意，reach 後面不需要加介系詞。
> 而「售後服務」的英文是 after-sales service。

隨堂測驗 A

請依 CD 所播放的內容，完成下列對話。

🔘 Track 11

試試這樣說～ | 牛刀小試！

1 A: 喂，請問約翰厄文先生在嗎？
B: 在。**請稍候。**

A: Hello. Is Mr. John Irving there?
B: Yes. _____

2 A: 喂，**可以請**莎莉史奈德小姐**聽電話嗎**？
B: **請問您是哪位**？
A: 我是攝影師瑪莉亞。

A: Hello. _____
Ms. Sally Schneider?
B: _____
A: This is Maria, the photographer.

3 A: 喂，**請問**哈利斯先生方便講電話嗎？
B: 請稍等一下，我去看看。

A: Hello. _____
B: Just a moment, please. I'll go check.

4 A: **請問您有什麼事**？
B: 我是為了與費雪先生的會面打來的。
A: 好的。**請稍候，別掛斷。**

A: _____
B: I'm calling about my meeting with Mr.
Fisher.
A: OK. _____

5 A: 請問要如何聯繫到凱莉小姐？
B: **她的分機**是 302，我幫您轉接。

A: _____ Ms. Kelly?
B: _____ is 302.
I'll put you through.

請聽 CD 完成下列三組不同情境的對話。

🔊**Track 12**

1 你現在要找東西銀行的伯恩斯小姐，但是接電話的是別人，請試著讓對方幫你轉接。

A: 感謝您來電東西銀行。請問您需要什麼協助？

B: 我想要找伯恩斯小姐。

A: 請問您是要找海瑟伯恩斯小姐嗎？

B: 是的，就是**負責**企業金融部的那位女士。

A: 好，請稍等。

A: Thank you for calling East-West Bank. How may I help you?

B: _____

A: Are you looking for Ms. Heather Burns?

B: Yes, the lady _____ the corporate banking section.

A: OK, hang on just a minute.

🔊**Track 13**

2 有人來電找電話中的尼爾森先生，請詢問對方目的後告知他正在講電話。

A: 喂，我是伊莎貝爾比格羅。請問尼爾森先生在嗎？

B: 請問您有什麼事嗎？

A: 我是為了我之前詢問過的資訊打來。我想知道什麼時候可以收到答覆。

B: 好，**可以請您不要掛稍等一下嗎**？噢，尼爾森先生正在講電話。

A: 好，那我待會兒再打來。

B: 好的，再見。

A: Hello, my name is Isabel Bigelow. Is Mr. Nelson there?

B: _____

A: I'm calling about the information I've requested. I was wondering when I could expect to get it.

B: OK. _____ Oh, Mr. Nelson is on another line.

A: All right. I'll call him later.

B: OK, bye-bye.

Track 14

3　聽說艾倫帕克剛剛有打電話來，趕快回電吧。如果他現在不能講電話，就試著問他的分機號碼。

A: 喂，我是蔡海倫。請問您需要什麼協助？

B: 您好，我想找艾倫帕克。**可以幫我轉接嗎**？

A: 不好意思，他現在不在辦公室裡。

B: **請問他的分機幾號**？我待會兒再找他。

A: 是 202。

B: 多謝。

A: Hello, this is Helen Tsai. How may I help you?

B: Hi, I'm trying to reach Alan Parker. _____

A: I'm sorry, but he's not in his office now.

B: _____ I'll call him later.

A: It's 202.

B: Thanks a lot.

Answers

無法接聽電話時

He's not here right now.

〉〉請跟著 Kevin 一起練習用英語處理無法接聽電話的各種狀況。

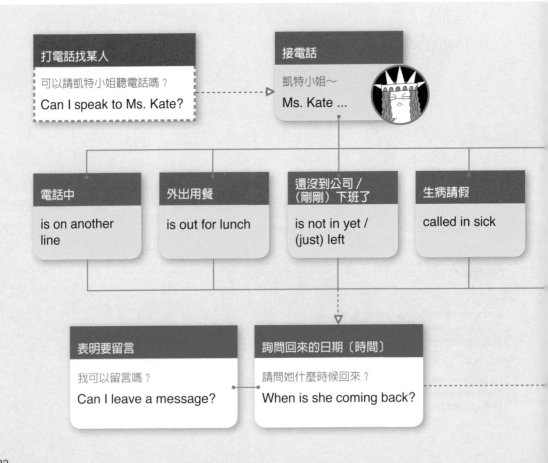

打電話找某人

可以請凱特小姐聽電話嗎？

Can I speak to Ms. Kate?

接電話

凱特小姐～

Ms. Kate ...

電話中

is on another line

外出用餐

is out for lunch

還沒到公司 / （剛剛）下班了

is not in yet / (just) left

生病請假

called in sick

表明要留言

我可以留言嗎？

Can I leave a message?

詢問回來的日期〔時間〕

請問她什麼時候回來？

When is she coming back?

Kate 老師的重點提示

◆ 沒有上班 **not in** 這裡的 in 是「有來上班、在辦公室」的意思。

◆ 會議中 **in a meeting** 口語上不需要用到 conference 這個字來指會議，meeting 就夠了。

◆ 沒有班 / 不值班 **off duty** 相反地，值班 / 工作中就是 on duty。

◆ 休一天假 **a day off** 依此類推，休兩天為 two days off，休三天則為 three days off，動詞用 take。

◆ 休長假中 **on vacation** vacation 一字指天數較長的假期。

◆ 請病假 **call in sick** He/She called in sick. 就是「他 / 她今天請病假」的意思。

◆ 家裡有急事 **family emergency** 一般而言，因家人生病等而缺勤或早退都是用 family emergency 來說明。

◆ 在講電話 **be on another line** 若要表達「他正在電話中」，不要說 He's talking to somebody else. 這樣比較不道地；簡單地說 He's on another line. 就好。

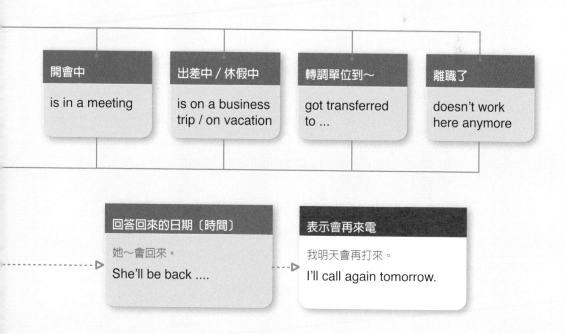

開會中	出差中 / 休假中	轉調單位到～	離職了
is in a meeting	is on a business trip / on vacation	got transferred to ...	doesn't work here anymore

回答回來的日期〔時間〕	表示會再來電
她～會回來。 She'll be back	我明天會再打來。 I'll call again tomorrow.

電話英語通關句 TOP 10

工作忙的時候總是會接到找不在座位上的人的電話！已經下班的上司也好，出差中的前輩也好，請病假的後輩也好……無法接聽電話的原因「百百款」。此時要怎樣用英文傳達呢？

Please ~ leave your message

🔊 Track 15

He's not here right now.
他現在不在。

因為中文會說不在「座位」上，所以很容易就會講成 He's not at his seat.，但是其實只要說他現在「不在 (here)」就好。可以說 He's not here. 或 He's not in the office at the moment.。如果他是去吃飯了的話，就說 He's out for lunch.（他去吃午飯了）。

A Hello, is Mr. Watson there?
喂，請問華森先生在嗎？

B No, he's not here right now.
他現在不在。

She's on another line.
她現在電話中。

這裡的 line 是指「電話線」。如果來電是找同公司的職員，也可回答 He's on line 2.（他在 2 線上）。

· I'm sorry, but his line is busy at the moment.
不好意思，他現在電話中。

· Shall I have her call you back?
要我請她回電給您嗎？

· Could you call back later?
可以請您待會兒再打來嗎？

· Would you hold on for a moment?
可以請您等一下嗎？

34

He just left.

他剛離開。

英語中並沒有像中文「上班」、「下班」這樣單一個詞就能達意，大多要用 go to work（上班）以及 leave one's work/office（下班）等片語來表示。不過，也可以像 He left five minutes ago.（他五分鐘前下班了）這樣提供一些詳細的情報，或是說 You just missed him. He just left. 傳達出對方剛剛才下班，可惜錯過了時機的感覺。而「還沒上班」就是 He's not in yet.。

> A　Is Mr. Ian Blair there?
> 請問伊安布萊爾先生在嗎？
>
> B　Oh, he just left.
> 噢，他剛下班。

She called in sick.

她請病假。

生病要請假時一般會打電話給公司，因此「請病假」就是 call in sick。接到打來找請病假同事的電話時就這樣回答吧。

> A　Hello, this is Sunny Lee at Microsoft. Could I speak to Ms. Wendy O'Connor?
> 喂，我是微軟的李桑妮。可以請溫蒂歐康納小姐聽電話嗎？
>
> B　Oh, she called in sick today.
> 噢，她今天請病假。

He's off today.

他今天請假。

off 是從 on duty「值班」/ off duty「不值班、沒有班」來的。

- He's taking a day off today.
  他今天請一天假。(= He's taking today off.)

- I was off yesterday.
  我昨天請假。

- Are you taking tomorrow off?
  你明天要請假嗎？

He's in a meeting.

他在開會。

會議「中」不用 during，請牢記 "in" a meeting 這樣的說法。之後與對方通到電話時也只要說 I was in a meeting.（我剛剛在開會）就好。

A Hello. I'm looking for Mr. Frank Cleary.
喂，我想找法蘭柯利瑞先生。

B He's in a meeting right now.
他現在在開會。

She's on a business trip.

她出差去了。

出差就是 on a business trip。注意，介系詞須用 on，這是從 on a trip「旅行中」／ on vacation「休假中」延伸出來的。

A Is Ms. Jones there?
請問瓊斯小姐在嗎？

B I'm sorry, but she's on a business trip to Hsinchu. She'll be back on Thursday though.
不好意思，她去新竹出差了，不過星期四就會回來。

He's on a two-week vacation.

他休兩個星期的假。

「兩週」作名詞用時，因爲是複數，所以字尾要加 s：two weeks；作形容詞「兩週的」使用時則須用單數形：two-week。只要記住 on vacation 此片語，前面形容長度的詞彙可任意變換。

· He's on vacation.
他休假去了。

· I went on vacation to Spain last summer.
我去年夏天到西班牙度假。

She got transferred to the Tainan branch.

她轉調到台南分公司去了。

transfer 是「遷移」的意思,若指學生為「轉學」,若指上班族則為「轉調(去另一個工作地點)」。注意,此處並非換工作之意,而是指仍隸屬於同一家公司但是轉去不同分店或辦公室。

· She moved to our branch in Tokyo.
  她調到東京分公司了。

· She has been transferred to our headquarters in Seattle.
  她已經轉調去西雅圖總部了。

He doesn't work here anymore.

他已經離職了。

當接到打電話來找已經離職的同事時,這是最簡單的回答方式。或者也可以說 He's not with us anymore.。此外,即使是被解雇的,也請避免說 He got fired.。

A Is Mr. Spelling there?
   請問史貝靈先生在嗎?

B Mr. Spelling doesn't work here anymore.
   史貝靈先生離職了。

🔊 **Track 16**

fire 和 quit 的差別

fire 是被公司解雇,而 quit 則是員工主動提出辭呈,意思完全不同。另外,資遣是 layoff (動詞為 lay off),榮譽退休則叫 honorary retirement。

· We know you've sold company secrets. You're fired.
  我們知道你出賣公司機密,你被解雇了。

· I quit my job today! I couldn't stand my boss anymore.
  我今天辭職了!我再也受不了我的老闆。

· My husband got laid off during the economic crisis.
  我先生在經濟危機時被資遣了。

核心句型練習

請確實開口反覆練習，讓自己熟悉這些句型。　　 ◐**Track 17**

史貝靈先生～。（說明無法接電話的原因）

Mr. Spelling is ⬭⬭⬭⬭⬭⬭⬭⬭⬭.

① not here right now　現在不在
② not in yet　還沒來
③ in a meeting　在開會

> 如果一定要表達「他現在不方便接電話」，可以說 I'm sorry, but he's not available now.。不過如果他「現在不在」或是「下班了」，就已經充分表示他現在不能接電話，因此並不需要講得那麼長。

史密斯小姐～。

Ms. Smith is on ⬭⬭⬭⬭⬭⬭⬭⬭⬭.

① a business trip　出差
② vacation for a week　休一週的假
③ maternity leave　休產假

> leave 和 vacation 一樣，亦為假別的一種，而 maternity leave 則指為了生產或育兒而請休的長假。

隨堂測驗 A

請依 CD 所播放的內容，完成下列對話。

Track 18

試試這樣説～　　　　　　　　　　　牛刀小試！

1 A: 喂，我想找葛瑞絲希爾小姐。
　 B: 她現在**在中國出差**。

　 A: Hello, can I speak to Ms. Grace Hill?
　 B: She's _____ to China.

2 A: 喂，請問威廉斯先生在嗎？
　 B: 噢，他這週**休假**。

　 A: Hello? Is Mr. Williams there?
　 B: Oh, he's _____ this week.

3 A: 喂，我是 C.A.N. 製片公司的亞綸，我想找瓊安納雅克。
　 B: 她**現在不在**。

　 A: Hello. This is Aaron calling from C.A.N. Productions. I'd like to speak to Joanna Ark, please.
　 B: She's _____.

4 A: 我是布蘭登威廉斯，請問陳先生出差回來了嗎？
　 B: 還沒，**他下週一會進公司**。

　 A: My name is Brandon Williams. Is Mr. Chen back from his business trip yet?
　 B: Not yet. _____

5 A: 我想找法蘭克先生。
　 B: 不好意思，他**不在這裡工作了**。

　 A: I'm looking for Mr. Frank.
　 B: I'm sorry, but he _____ _____ anymore.

請聽 CD 完成下列三組不同情境的對話。

🔘Track 19

1 有人打電話來找出差中的理查,請跟對方說理查明天會進公司。

A: **感謝您來電**菲澤保險公司。

B: 你好,請問理查利德先生在嗎?

A: **不好意思,他目前正在出差。**

B: 噢,是喔?他什麼時候回來?

A: **他明天會進公司。**

A: _____ Frasier Insurance.

B: Hi, is Mr. Richard Reed there?

A: _____

B: Oh, really? When is he coming back?

A: _____

🔘Track 20

2 有人打電話來找開會中的葛菲斯,請對方十分鐘之後再來電。

A: 喂,您好。我找葛菲斯先生。

B: **他在開會。**您要留言嗎?

A: 會議要開多久?

B: 他大概十分鐘之後就開完了。**可以請您待會兒再打來嗎?**

A: 好的。

A: Hello. Could I speak to Mr. Griffith?

B: _____ Would you like to leave a message?

A: How long will it take?

B: He'll be done in about 10 minutes. _____

A: OK. I will.

🔊**Track 21**

3 請試著打電話給卡特小姐，如果她不在，就說你明天會再來電。

A: 喂，**我是喬霍華**。請問卡特小姐在嗎？

B: 抱歉，她現在不在。

A: 你知道她在哪裡嗎？

B: 知道，她今天請病假。要我請她回電給您嗎？

A: 不用了，**我明天再打來**。

B: 好，再見。

A: Hello. _____ Is Ms. Carter there?

B: Sorry. She's not here now.

A: Do you have any idea where she is?

B: Yes. She called in sick today. Shall I have her call you back?

A: No. _____

B: OK. Goodbye.

Answers

隨堂測驗 A

1 on a business trip   2 on vacation   3 not here right now   4 He'll be back next Monday.
5 doesn't work here

隨堂測驗 B

1 Thank you for calling / I'm sorry, but he's on a business trip right now. / He'll be back tomorrow.
2 He's in a meeting. / Could you call back later?   3 This is Joe Howard. / I'll call again tomorrow.

留言

Would you like me to take a message?

〉〉請跟著 Kevin 一起練習用英語留言的各種說法。

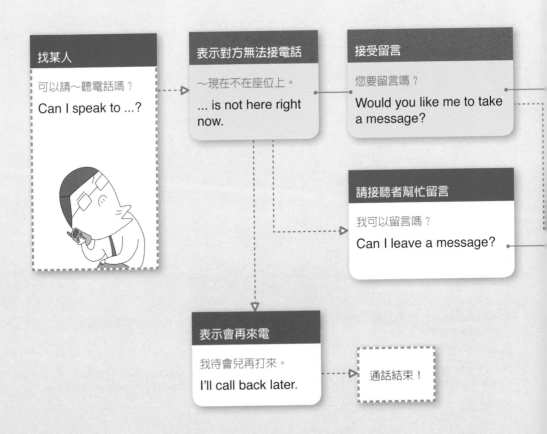

找某人

可以請～聽電話嗎？

Can I speak to ...?

表示對方無法接電話

～現在不在座位上。

... is not here right now.

接受留言

您要留言嗎？

Would you like me to take a message?

請接聽者幫忙留言

我可以留言嗎？

Can I leave a message?

表示會再來電

我待會兒再打來。

I'll call back later.

通話結束！

Kate 老師的重點提示

◆ 留言 **leave a message** 動詞用 leave。

◆ 接受留言 **take a message** 動詞用 take，而不用 receive。

◆ 語音留言 **voice message** 也常聽到 voice mail 這個說法。

◆ 傳達留言 **give the message** 因為是傳達訊息「給」別人，所以在對象前直接加上介系詞 to 就好。

◆ 留言用的紙 **something to write on** 若要說「留言用的筆」，則是 something to write with。

◆ 務必要 **make sure** 此片語用以表示一定會執行 sure 後接的行動。

◆ 一有時間就 **at one's earliest convenience** 語意類似 as soon as possible，亦十分常見。

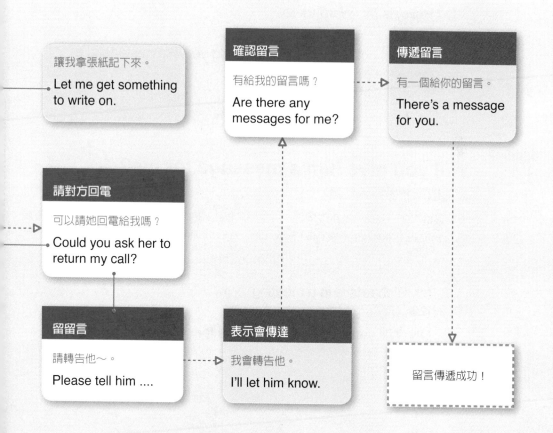

讓我拿張紙記下來。
Let me get something to write on.

確認留言
有給我的留言嗎？
Are there any messages for me?

傳遞留言
有一個給你的留言。
There's a message for you.

請對方回電
可以請她回電給我嗎？
Could you ask her to return my call?

留留言
請轉告他～。
Please tell him ....

表示會傳達
我會轉告他。
I'll let him know.

留言傳遞成功！

當有人來電找不在的同事時，可詢問對方是否有訊息要傳達。自己打電話的時候也是一樣，對象不在時無須慌張，只要熟記請人協助留言的下列各種說法就 OK。

🔊Track 22

01 Would you like me to take a message?

您要留言嗎？

注意，也可說 Can I take a message? 或 Do you want to leave a message?，但是不要講成 May I take your message?，老外一般不會這麼說。

A Hello, is Mr. Ward there?
喂，請問沃德先生在嗎？

B No, he's not here right now. Would you like me to take a message?
不，他現在不在。您要留言嗎？

---

02 Will you give him a message for me?

您可以幫我留言給他嗎？

要留給不在的人員時就請這麼說。可以用比較正式的 I'd like to ... 句型，即 I'd like to leave a message (please).，或 Can I leave a message (for him)?。

A Mr. Richards is in a meeting.
理查茲先生正在開會。

B OK. Will you give him a message for me?
好。可以請你幫我留言給他嗎？

Let me get something to write on.
讓我拿張紙記下來。

此說法比 Let me get a piece of paper. 更自然。而若是要問「有筆嗎?」,比起平鋪直述 Do you have a pen? , Do you have something to write with? 這個句子則更貼近老外口吻。

> A I'd like to leave a message for Dr. Walzac, please.
> 我想留言給瓦茲克博士。
>
> B OK, just a moment. Let me get something to write on.
> 好的,請稍等,讓我拿張紙記下來。

Please tell him Luke Nelson called.
請轉告他路克尼爾森有來電。

我們最常留言的內容應該就是「請告訴他~有打電話來」吧,如果跟接電話的人很熟的話,只要說 This is Luke Nelson. 對方就應該明白了。

> A Mr. Willis is in a meeting right now. Would you like to leave a message?
> 威利斯先生現在在開會。您要留言嗎?
>
> B Tell him Luke Nelson called, please. He has my number.
> 請告訴他路克尼爾森有來電。他有我的電話。

Could you ask her to return my call?
可以請她回電給我嗎?

return a (phone) call 即回撥未接來電,或者也可簡單說 call back。

- Would you please ask him to call me as soon as he gets off the phone?
  可以請他講完電話之後馬上回電給我嗎?

- Could you ask her to return my call at her earliest convenience?
  可以請她方便的時候盡快回電給我嗎?

I'll call again later.

我待會兒再打來。

這個句子當中的動詞也可以用 try 替換，即 I'll try again later.；或者也可像 I'll call again around three o'clock.（我在三點左右會再打來）這樣進一步點出特定的時間。

A Shall I have him call you back?
要請他回電給您嗎？

B Oh, no. He doesn't know my number. I'll call again later.
噢，不用了。他不知道我的號碼，我待會兒會再打來。

I'll let him know.

我會轉告他。

當然也可以說 I'll give him the message.，不過像主題句那樣才是更自然的口語說法。

A Can I take a message?
您要留言嗎？

B OK. Please tell him Ian Malcolm called.
好，請轉告他伊安馬爾康有來電。

A All right. I'll let him know first thing tomorrow morning.
好的，我明天一早就會轉告他。

Are there any messages for me?

有給我的留言嗎？

也可簡略地問 Any messages for me? 或 Any messages?。

A Good morning! Any messages for me?
早！有給我的留言嗎？

B Yes, Mrs. Paltrow. I have two messages for you.
有的，派特蘿女士，有兩個給您的留言。

There's a message for you.

有一個給你的留言。

要表達「給～」的訊息,直接用 for「爲了」即可。

A Mr. Buttermaker, there's a message for you.
伯特美克先生,你有一個留言。

B Oh, yeah? Who's it from?
是喔?是誰留的?

I left a message for you yesterday.

昨天我留了一個留言給你。

這是用來確認當事人是否有收到留言的說法,還有以下其他幾種表達方式。

· Did you get my message?
你有收到我的留言嗎?

· I got your message, thank you.
我收到你的留言了。謝謝。

· I left a voice message on your cell. Did you get it?
我在你的手機留了一則語音訊息。你有聽嗎?

return 和 get back 的差別

return a call 是回撥給沒有接到的電話,而 get back to someone 則是當下有接到電話但稍後會再打給對方的意思。如果是看到手機上有未接來電而回電,則應該說 return a call。

請確實開口反覆練習，讓自己熟悉這些句型。　　🎧**Track 23**

有～的留言嗎？
Are there any messages _____?

① for me　給我
② from Mr. Kent　肯特先生留
③ from Smallville　斯摩維爾公司留

from 一個介系詞即可表達「～留」的，不需要用複雜的句式，例如 a message left by ... 等。

請轉告他～。
Please tell him _____.

① that Clark Mays called　克拉克梅斯有來電
② to call Dr. Halloway's office　回電給哈羅威博士的辦公室
③ that his flight reservation has been made　他的班機訂位已經完成

也可以說 Please let him know (that) ...，若要更有禮貌，則可用 Could you tell him (that) ... 或 Could you please let him know (that) ... 這兩種句型。

隨堂測驗 A

請依 CD 所播放的內容，完成下列對話。

Track 24

 試試這樣說～

 牛刀小試！

1 A: 喂你好，我想找克拉克先生。
B: 他在開會，您要**留言**嗎？

A: Hello, can I speak to Mr. Clark?
B: He's in a meeting. Would you like me
_____?

2 A: 喂，請問羅斯福小姐在嗎？
B: 她今天休假。您要留言嗎？
A: 好，我是珍恩凱莉。可以請她**回電給我**嗎？

A: Hello? Is Ms. Roosevelt there?
B: Oh, she's off today. Can I take a message?
A: Yes, my name is Jane Carrey. Could you
ask her _____?

3 A: 喂，我是廖泰森。昨天**我有留言給**基曼小姐。
B: 噢，有的。我剛剛把留言給她了。

A: Hello. My name is Tyson Liao.
_____ Ms. Kidman
yesterday.
B: Oh, yes. I just gave the message to her.

4 A: 我是班崔普。請告訴李先生**我有打電話**來談會議的事。
B: 沒問題。

A: My name is Ben Tripp. Please tell Mr. Lee
_____ about the meeting.
B: Sure.

5 A: **有給我的留言嗎**？
B: 有，有三個留言。

A: _____
B: Yes, there are three messages for you.

49

隨堂測驗

請聽 CD 完成下列三組不同情境的對話。

🎧 Track 25

1 請打電話給愛麗絲艾凡斯小姐,她不在的話請試著留言。

A: 你好,可以請愛麗絲艾凡斯小姐聽電話嗎?

B: 她出差去了。您要留言嗎?

A: 噢,好。**請告訴她林建文有來電。**

B: 好的,她一回來我就會跟她說。她有您的電話嗎?

A: **有,她有。**

A: Hi, can I talk to Ms. Alice Evans?

B: She's on a business trip. Can I take a message?

A: Oh, sure. _____

B: OK, I'll give your message to her as soon as she comes back. Does she have your number?

A: _____

🎧 Track 26

2 有人打電話來找不在的金東尼,請試著問對方要不要留言。

A: 喂,我是莎拉波諾。請問金東尼先生在嗎?

B: **他現在不在。您要留言嗎?**

A: 好,請告訴他他的健檢報告出來了。

B: 好的。請問您的電話號碼是?

A: 我的電話是 02-468101。

B: 好的,**我會轉告他。**

A: Hello, my name is Sarah Bono. Is Mr. Tony Kim there?

B: _____

A: Yes, could you let him know that his test results are in?

B: Sure. May I have your number?

A: Yes, it's 02-468101.

B: OK. _____

Track 27

3　留言給山姆卻遲遲沒有消息，請試著確認山姆是否有收到留言。

A: 喂，山姆，**你有收到我的留言嗎**？

B: 留言？什麼留言？

A: **我昨天有留言給你**。你沒收到嗎？

B: 沒有，我沒收到。你說了什麼？

A: 我想問你蘿拉的電話號碼。

B: 噢……她的電話是 0983-119723。

A: 謝了。

A: Hello, Sam. _____

B: Message? What message?

A: _____

　　Didn't you get it?

B: No, I didn't. What did you say?

A: I asked you for Laura's phone number.

B: Oh ... it's 0983-119723.

A: Thanks a lot.

A. 請利用括弧內的提示填空以完成句子。 Track 28

1 A: 喂？
  B: 喂，**我是業務部的查爾斯**。(Charles / the sales department)
  A: Hello?
  B: Hello. _____

2 A: 感謝您來電葛雷普企業。**請問您需要什麼協助？** (help)
  B: 喂，**可以請湯米李先生聽電話嗎？** (Can I ...? / Tommy Lee)
  A: Thank you for calling the Grape Co. _____
  B: Hello. _____

3 A: 請問哈利伯特非爾先生在嗎？
  B: 在，請稍候，**我幫您轉接**。(put ... through)
  A: Is Harry Butterfield there?
  B: Yes, just a moment. _____

4 A: **可以請問您有什麼事嗎？** (May I ...? / concerning)
  B: 噢，我是為了明天跟萊德先生的會議打來。
  A: _____
  B: Oh, I'm calling about my meeting with Mr. Ryder tomorrow.

5 A: **您要留言嗎？** (Would you like me ...?)
  B: 不用，謝謝。我待會再打來。
  A: _____
  B: No, thanks. I'll call back later.

B. 請將下列對話中文部分翻譯成英文。

A: Ryan Jones. Thank you for your call.

B: Hello. ① 可以請傑森史考特先生聽電話嗎？

A: ② 他休假去了。

B: Then can I leave a message?

A: Sure.

B: Thank you. My name is Nicole Postman, and ③ 我的電話是 2345-6789.

A: OK. Let me verify that. It's 2345-6789, right?

B: Yes. ④ 麻煩請他打電話給我。

A: OK.

Ans.

① _____   ② _____

③ _____   ④ _____

A: Thank you for calling East-West Bank. ⑤ 請問您需要什麼協助？

B: Hello. ⑥ 請問要如何聯繫到貝克先生？

A: Are you looking for Mr. James Baker?

B: Yes, the man in the corporate banking section.

A: OK. ⑦ 他的分機是121。

B: Thank you.

A: ⑧ 需要我為您轉接嗎？

B: Yes, please.

Ans.

⑤ _____   ⑥ _____

⑦ _____   ⑧ _____

C. 請和 Kate 老師一起模擬接打電話,做雙向問答練習。

* 本單元錄音內容共有兩遍,第一遍的每一句之間保留了較長的間隔,請利用空檔做跟讀練習;練習完之後,請再聽一遍正常語速的版本。

🔊 **Track 31**

接聽電話

請扮演 Kevin 的角色,練習接 Kate 的電話。

Kevin :K&G 貿易公司,我是林建文。請問您需要什麼協助?

Kate :Hello, is Henry Fielding in?

Kevin :請問您哪位?

Kate :This is Kate Kim calling from Bridget Trading Company.

Kevin :請稍候,我將為您轉接。

Kate :Thank you.

🔊 **Track 32**

撥打電話

請扮演 Kevin 的角色,試著打電話給 Kate。

Kevin :喂,可以請威利斯先生聽電話嗎?

Kate :Mr. Willis is on another line.

Kevin :我可以留言嗎?

Kate :Sure.

Kevin :可以請他方便的時候盡快回電給我嗎?
我是林建文,他有我的電話。

Kate :OK. I'll let him know.

* 全篇對話之中文翻譯請左右兩頁對照參閱。

撥打電話

接下來換你練習打電話給 Kate。

Kate : K&G Trading Company. This is Kate. How may I help you?

Kevin : 喂，請問亨利菲爾丁先生在嗎？

Kate : May I ask who's calling, please?

Kevin : 我是布利吉貿易公司的林建文。

Kate : Just a moment, please. I'll transfer your call.

Kevin : 謝謝。

接聽電話

再來請練習接 Kate 的電話。

Kate : Hello. Is Mr. Willis available?

Kevin : 威利斯先生現在電話中。

Kate : Can I leave a message?

Kevin : 好的。

Kate : Could you ask him to return my call as soon as possible?
My name is Kate Kim, and he has my number.

Kevin : 好的，我會轉告他。

複習時間 Answers

A

1 This is Charles from the sales department.
2 How may I help you?
  Can I speak to Mr. Tommy Lee?
3 I'll put you through.
4 May I ask what this is concerning?
5 Would you like me to take a message?

B

① Can I talk to Mr. Jason Scott?
③ my number is 2345-6789
⑤ How may I help you?
⑦ His extension is 121.

② He's on vacation now.
④ Please ask him to call me.
⑥ How can I reach Mr. Baker?
⑧ Would you like me to put you through?

翻譯
留言
A: 我是萊恩瓊斯,感謝您的來電。
B: 喂,可以請傑森史考特先生聽電話嗎?
A: 他休假去了。
B: 那我可以留言嗎?
A: 好的。
B: 謝謝。我是妮可波茲曼,我的電話是 2345-6789。
A: 好,我確認一下,是 2345-6789 對嗎?
B: 沒錯。麻煩請他打電話給我。
A: 好的。

轉接
A: 感謝您來電東西銀行。請問您需要什麼協助?
B: 喂,請問要如何聯繫到貝克先生?
A: 請問您是要找詹姆士貝克嗎?
B: 是的,企業金融部的。
A: 好的,他的分機是 121。
B: 謝謝。
A: 需要我為您轉接嗎?
B: 好的,麻煩了。

Week 2

商務篇①

是……

腿再併攏一點，
要親切……

約定會面

I'd like to make an appointment.

〉〉請跟著 Kevin 一起練習打電話與商務對象安排會面。

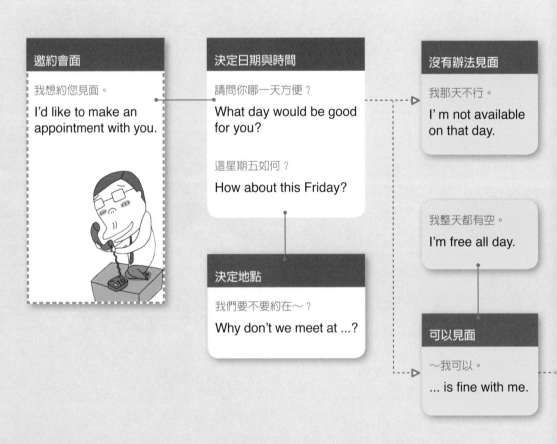

邀約會面

我想約您見面。

I'd like to make an appointment with you.

決定日期與時間

請問你哪一天方便？

What day would be good for you?

這星期五如何？

How about this Friday?

決定地點

我們要不要約在～？

Why don't we meet at ...?

沒有辦法見面

我那天不行。

I'm not available on that day.

我整天都有空。

I'm free all day.

可以見面

～我可以。

... is fine with me.

Kate 老師的重點提示

◆ 約定 **appointment (n.)** reservation 和 appointment 的用法很類似，但是意思並不一樣。make a reservation 通常是指預訂「空間」，例如一張桌子（餐廳的座位）、一間飯店的房間等；make an appointment 則通常是指預約某人的「時間」，例如上髮廊弄頭髮、看醫生等。

◆ 約定見面 **make an appointment**

◆ 取消約定 **cancel an appointment**

◆ 約定改期 **reschedule an appointment**

◆ ～如何？ **How about ...?** 與人約定見面時最基本的句型。

◆ 有空 **free (adj.)** 這個字除了有「自由」的意思之外，也可表示「有時間」。

◆ 不方便 **not good** 如果不方便赴約的話，就說〔日期 / 時間〕is not good for me.，簡單且有禮貌。

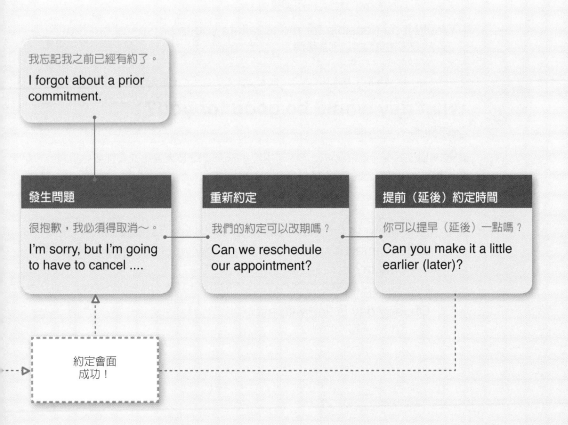

我忘記我之前已經有約了。
I forgot about a prior commitment.

發生問題

很抱歉，我必須得取消～。
I'm sorry, but I'm going to have to cancel ....

重新約定

我們的約定可以改期嗎？
Can we reschedule our appointment?

提前（延後）約定時間

你可以提早（延後）一點嗎？
Can you make it a little earlier (later)?

約定會面
成功！

電話英語通關句 TOP 10

商場上拜訪客戶或負責人之前，先約定時間不但是禮貌也是常識。用英語確認雙方行程以決定日期、時間與地點這件事好像很複雜，但是其實非常簡單！

🎧 Track 33

I'd like to make an appointment.
我想約個時間跟您見面。

商務場合的約定會面在英文是用 appointment 這個字，「約定時間見面」即 make an appointment，口語上也常聽到有人說 set up an appointment。

· If you don't mind, I'd like to meet you sometime next week.
  如果您不介意的話，我想約您下週碰面。

· Would it be possible for me to talk to you in person about that?
  可以跟您直接見面談談那件事嗎？

What day would be good for you?
請問你哪一天方便？

比起 What day is good for you?，在句中使用 would 聽起來會比較委婉並尊重對方。另外，也可以用 What time should we make it? 來詢問。

A I'm calling to let you know that we'd like to schedule a second interview with you. What day would be good for you to come in?
  我來電是要告訴你我們想跟你約第二次的面試。請問你哪一天方便過來？

B Oh, any day is fine with me.
  噢，我哪一天都可以。

How about next Friday at 4 p.m.?

下週五下午四點如何？

How about ...? 就是「～怎麼樣？」的意思，用以提議或詢問意願。如果對方回覆的時間自己也沒問題，就回答 That would be fine with me.；若不行就在 I'm sorry but ... 後面簡單說出原因，然後再用 How about ..., instead? 進一步與對方協調。

A How about next Friday at 4 p.m.?
下週五下午四點如何？

B That would be fine with me.
我可以。

I'm free all day.

我整天都有空。

若要表達「有時間、什麼時候都 OK」，就用 free 這個字。free 除了「自由的、免費的」之外，也可指「沒有別的事、時間很自由」。

A I'm free all day Wednesday. Any time will be fine.
我禮拜三整天都有空，什麼時候都行。

B Great. How about 1:30?
太好了。那一點半怎麼樣？

I'm not available on that day.

我那天不行。

not available / unavailable 表示沒有時間。另外，如同前面學過的，依對話內容，He/She's not available. 也可指「無法接聽電話」。

· I'm afraid I can't make it on that day.
那天我恐怕沒辦法。

· I'm sorry, but tomorrow is a busy day for me. Can we meet another day?
抱歉，我明天很忙。我們可以改天碰面嗎？

I'm sorry, but I'm going to have to cancel tomorrow's lunch.

很抱歉，我必須得取消明天的午餐約定。

像這樣取消約定是相當有禮貌的，而 I'm going to ... 則讓句子更有口語的感覺，如果只說 I have to cancel tomorrow's lunch. 聽起來會有點生硬。

A　Hi, Robert. How are you doing?
嗨，羅伯特，你好嗎？

B　Good, good. Hey, listen. I'm sorry, but I'm going to have to cancel tomorrow's lunch.
很好。嘿，我跟你說，不好意思我得取消明天的午餐約定。

Can we reschedule our appointment?

我們的約定可以改期嗎？

字首 re- 加在動詞前面表示「重新～」，因此 reschedule (an appointment) 即「重新約」之意。

A　I'm sorry I have to cancel the appointment. So, can we reschedule it?
抱歉我得取消會面。那，我們可以另外再約時間嗎？

B　Oh, then how about next Monday instead?
噢，那改成下週一如何？

A　That would be fine with me.
下週一我可以。

I forgot about a prior commitment.

我忘記我之前已經有約了。

「更早之前做的約定」爲 prior commitment 或 previous engagement，「我那天另外有約了」則可以說 I have a prior commitment on that day.。

· Something urgent has come up.
突然有急事。

I'm going to be late for our appointment.

我會遲到一些。

如果會晚到也要記得先打電話告知會面對象。在開頭加上 I'm sorry. 的話更有禮貌。

· I'm sorry, but I can't get to your office by 1:30.
  很抱歉，我一點半之前趕不到你的辦公室。

· I just got out of a meeting, so I'm going to be late.
  我剛結束一個會議，所以可能會遲到。

· I'm afraid I can't make it on time. I'm stuck in traffic.
  很抱歉，我恐怕沒辦法準時到。我塞在路上。

Can you make it a little earlier?

你可以提早一點嗎？

此處 make it 即「準時到達」之意。如果是要詢問延遲的可能性，就用 later 取代 earlier。

> A Can you make it a little earlier? I forgot about a prior commitment that I have at noon.
> 可以請你早一點來嗎？我忘記我中午有另外一個約。
>
> B Sure! I can come over at ten. Would that be OK with you?
> 沒問題！我可以十點過去。那個時間你 OK 嗎？

約定會面 make it 很好用

🔊Track 34

不需要深究 make it 的 it 是指什麼，基本上，這個片語就是「準時到達」的意思，無論商務會面或日常約會都很常用。

· When can you make it? 你什麼時候會到？
· Can you make it at 6:15? 你六點十五分可以到嗎？
· I'm sorry, but I can't make it on time. 很抱歉我沒有辦法準時到。

核心句型練習

請確實開口反覆練習，讓自己熟悉這些句型。

如果可以的話，～

If possible,

① I'd like to make an appointment to meet you. 我想跟您約見面。
② I'd like to see you this week. 我這週想跟你碰面。
③ could you spare me about thirty minutes? 您能給我三十分鐘的時間嗎？

> if possible 即「如果可以～」之意，為 if it's possible 之
> 省略。同樣的省略用法還有 if (it's) necessary ...（有需
> 要的話～）。

很抱歉，～。

I'm sorry, but

① I'm going to have to cancel the appointment 我必須得取消會面
② I'd like to reschedule our appointment 我們的約定我想改期
③ I'm going to be late for my appointment 我的約定我會遲到

> 英語中 I'm sorry 後面經常跟著 but，用以緩衝語氣。第
> 二個句子裡的 "reschedule" our appointment 是「改期」
> 之意。

隨堂測驗 **A**

請依 CD 所播放的內容，完成下列對話。

🔵**Track 36**

試試這樣説～   牛刀小試！

1 A: 如果可以的話，我想跟你約下週二見面。
B: 好的。下午三點如何？

A: If it's OK with you, I'd like to meet you next Tuesday.
B: Sure. _____

2 A: 下禮拜可以跟你碰個面嗎？
B: 嗯，如果你禮拜五來的話，我可以請你吃午飯。
A: 很抱歉我那天不行。我之前已經有約了。

A: Can I _____?
B: Well, if you can come on Friday, I'll buy you lunch.
A: I'm sorry but I can't come that day.
   I _____.

3 A: 請跟他說，如果可以的話，我想把跟他碰面的時間延到下週二。
B: 好的，我會跟他說。

A: Please tell him that, _____,
   I'd like to postpone my meeting with him
   until next Tuesday.
B: OK. I'll let him know.

4 A: 所以，九點半你方便嗎？
B: 沒問題。你的辦公室見。

A: So, is 9:30 OK for you?
B: _____
   I'll see you at your office.

5 A: 這週六如何？
B: 週六我整天都有空。

A: How about this Saturday?
B: _____ Saturday.

65

請聽 CD 完成下列三組不同情境的對話。

🔘Track 37

1　請試著和薇薇安懷特取消會面，改到隔天。

A: 喂，我是薇薇安懷特。
B: 你好，我是建文。抱歉，我得取消下週四的會面。**我們可以改時間嗎？**
A: 沒問題，星期五如何？**你的行程怎麼樣？**
B: **星期五我可以。**一點如何？

A: Hello, Vivian White speaking.

B: Hi, this is Kevin. I'm sorry, but I'm going to have to cancel our

　　appointment on Thursday. _____

A: Sure, how about Friday? _____

B: _____ How about at one o'clock?

🔘Track 38

2　請試著跟霍華約見面。

A: 喂，霍華先生，我是克莉絲塔。
B: 克莉絲塔，嗨！妳好嗎？
A: 還不錯，霍華先生。如果你不介意的話，**我想這週找個時間跟您碰個面。**
B: 好啊。**星期三如何？**我十一點左右有空。
A: 那個時間我可以。那就星期三見。

A: Hello, Mr. Howard. This is Krista.

B: Krista, hi! How are you doing?

A: Not bad, Mr. Howard.

　　If you don't mind, _____

B: Sure. _____

　　I can see you at around eleven.

A: That would be fine with me. Then I'll see you on Wednesday.

⏺Track 39

3　馬克打電話來約碰面，時間上看來星期四的三點或明天整天會比較好。

A: 喂，陳太太，我是馬克威爾森。

B: 馬克你好。有什麼事嗎？

A: 我想跟您約個時間見面。**您什麼時候有空**？

B: 嗯……這禮拜四的三點怎麼樣？

A: 很抱歉，**我那天不行**。改明天如何？

B: 我明天整天都有空。

A: 太好了。十一點見面可以嗎？

B: 可以。**到時見**。

A: Hello, Mrs. Chen. This is Mark Wilson.

B: Hello, Mark. What can I do for you?

A: I'd like to make an appointment with you. _____

B: Well, how about this Thursday at three?

A: Sorry. _____ How about tomorrow instead?

B: I'm free all day tomorrow.

A: Great. Can I see you at eleven?

B: That's fine with me. _____

Week

2

詢問與回答

I have some questions about your product.

| 星期六第二堂課 |

〉〉請跟著 Kevin 一起練習用英語打電話做問答溝通。

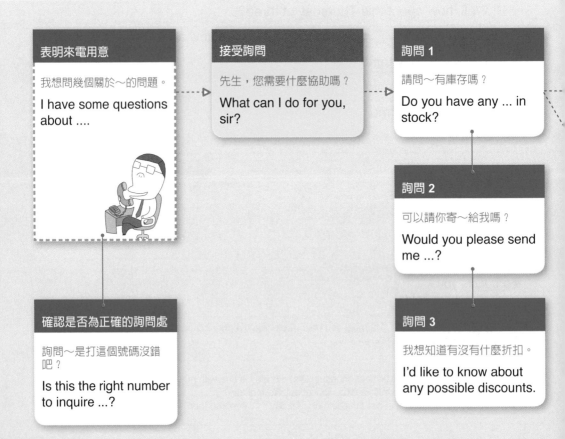

表明來電用意

我想問幾個關於～的問題。

I have some questions about ....

接受詢問

先生，您需要什麼協助嗎？

What can I do for you, sir?

詢問 1

請問～有庫存嗎？

Do you have any ... in stock?

確認是否為正確的詢問處

詢問～是打這個號碼沒錯吧？

Is this the right number to inquire ...?

詢問 2

可以請你寄～給我嗎？

Would you please send me ...?

詢問 3

我想知道有沒有什麼折扣。

I'd like to know about any possible discounts.

Kate 老師的重點提示

◆ 詢問 **inquiry (n.)** 正式的詢問用 inquiry，非正式的用 question。順帶一提，inquiry 是 inquire 的名詞形。注意，動詞與名詞的重音位置不一樣。（inquire 重音在第二音節，inquiry 重音則是在第一音節。）

◆ 更多的、進一步的訊息 **more/further information** 注意，information 不可數。

◆ 詢問關於～ **inquiry about/regarding ...** 相對之下，用 about 較口語。

◆ 客服人員 **customer service representative** 常聽到的語音「所有客服人員都在忙線中」就是 All our representatives are busy.。

◆ 請聯繫～ **please contact ...** 也可以說 please call ...，不過如果是「聯繫特定部門」，一般大都使用 contact。

◆ 別客氣請～ **feel free to ...** 帶有「請隨時／隨意～」的語感。

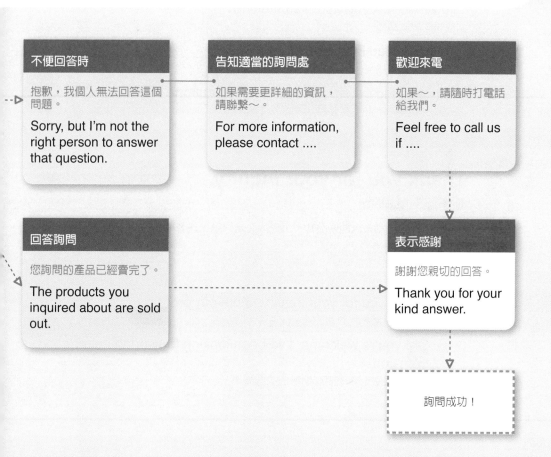

不便回答時

抱歉，我個人無法回答這個問題。

Sorry, but I'm not the right person to answer that question.

告知適當的詢問處

如果需要更詳細的資訊，請聯繫～。

For more information, please contact ....

歡迎來電

如果～，請隨時打電話給我們。

Feel free to call us if ....

回答詢問

您詢問的產品已經賣完了。

The products you inquired about are sold out.

表示感謝

謝謝您親切的回答。

Thank you for your kind answer.

詢問成功！

本課蒐集了詢問產品或是被詢問時可應用的各種表達方式。一般企業均設有專門負責客戶服務與產品諮詢的部門,而以下所介紹的句型都能幫得上忙!

🔴 Track 40

I have some questions about your product.

我想問幾個關於貴公司產品的問題。

如果你想要購買某公司的某項產品或者你的工作是採購,那就一定要記住這個最基本的句子。

- I'd like to ask you about something.
  我有問題想請教一下。

- I'm interested in one of your products.
  我對你們的一項產品有興趣。

- I'm calling to get some information about one of your products.
  我打來是想問一下有關你們一項產品的資訊。

Thank you for your inquiry.

感謝您來電詢問。

當接到顧客打電話來詢問產品時,可先以此句回應,或者用 Thank you for your interest in our product. 也很得體。

> A Thank you for your inquiry about our products, Mr. Clements.
> 感謝您來電詢問我們的產品,克萊門斯先生。
>
> B Oh, you're welcome. I've been looking forward to hearing from you.
> 噢,不客氣。我一直在期待您的回覆。

Is this the right number to inquire about products?

詢問產品是打這個號碼沒錯吧？

假設對方公司設有專門負責產品諮詢的部門時，可以這樣問來確認。

A Hello. Is this the right number to inquire about products?
喂，請問詢問產品是打到這邊嗎？

B Yes, ma'am. How can I help you?
是的，女士。您需要什麼幫助嗎？

For more information, please contact our customer service department.

如果需要更詳細的資訊，請與我們的客服部門聯繫。

「針對細節的問題」不能直接翻譯成 detailed questions，應用 more/further information 表示。

· Thank you for calling MAPS Design. For more information about our services, please press 9. The operator will assist you.
感謝您來電 MAPS 設計。如須更詳細的服務訊息，請按 9，由總機為您服務。

Do you have any A-100 models in stock?

請問 A-100 型號有庫存嗎？

「有現貨」可以說 have ... in stock，「沒有現貨」則為 out of stock。

A Do you have any YZ4789 models in stock?
請問你們 YZ4789 有貨嗎？

B How many would you like?
請問您需要多少？

The products you inquired about are sold out.
您詢問的產品已經賣完了。

sold out「賣完」，也可以說 out of stock「沒貨了」。

> A I'm sorry, but the products you inquired about are sold out.
>   很抱歉，您詢問的產品已經賣完了。
>
> B Oh, OK. Do you have something similar in stock?
>   噢，好吧。請問庫存裡有其他類似的產品嗎？

Would you please send me your catalog?
可以請你寄產品型錄給我嗎？

如果想要了解某項產品或某家公司，可以請對方寄廣告冊 (brochure) 或免費樣品 (free sample)。公司行號通常會將索取型錄的顧客視為潛在客戶 (promising customer)，並且親切地回應。

> A Would you please send me a free sample?
>   您可以寄一份免費樣品給我嗎？
>
> B Sure. Would you tell me where to send it?
>   沒問題。麻煩請告訴我寄送地址。

Sorry, but I'm not the right person to answer that question.
抱歉，我個人無法回答這個問題。

當來電者所詢問的問題自己不清楚狀況，或非本身負責職務而無法答覆時，這句話便能派上用場。

· My colleagues at the reservation desk will be able to answer your questions.
  我們訂位組的同仁將能夠回答您的問題。

09 Your inquiry was passed to the sales department.

您的問題已經轉達給業務部。

這裡的 pass 意指「傳送給～、轉達給～」。而業務部是 the sales department，建議放入不同部門名稱來練習。

A I called yesterday to ask about an item.
我昨天有打電話來問一個品項。

B Yes, your inquiry was passed to the marketing department yesterday.
是，您的問題昨天已經轉達給行銷部了。

10 Feel free to call us if you have any questions.

如果您有任何問題，請隨時打電話給我們。

若要表達「別客氣～、盡量～」之意，可以用 "feel free + to 不定詞" 此句型，也可以用 don't hesitate to ... 來替換 feel free to ...。hesitate 是「猶豫」的意思，don't hesitate ... 即「不要猶豫～」。

A Is there anything else I can help you with today?
今天還有什麼我能為您服務的嗎？

B No, that's it. Thanks.
沒有了，謝謝。

A If you have any more questions in the future, please feel free to call us.
如果您之後還有任何其他問題，請隨時來電。

各部門名稱
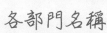

部門名和職稱一樣，每個公司可能會有一些不同，下面是一般常用的說法。

人資部 human resources department　公關部 public relations department
總務部 general affairs department　廣告部 advertising department
會計部 accounting department　企畫部 planning department
研發部 R&D department　行銷部 marketing department

請確實開口反覆練習，讓自己熟悉這些句型。　　　　🔘**Track 41**

我想問一個關於～的問題。
I have a question about ⬭⬭⬭⬭⬭⬭⬭⬭.

① the prices of your scanners　你們掃描機價格
② the condition of the digital camera that I purchased　我購買的數位相機的狀況
③ how to use a photo printer　照片列印機使用方法

> 也可以 inquiry 取代 question，不過如果是正式的詢問，用 inquiry 會更適當。第 2 句裡的 purchased 也可以 buy 的過去分詞 bought 替換。

您詢問的產品～。
The products you inquired about ⬭⬭⬭⬭⬭⬭⬭⬭.

① are out of stock right now　現在沒貨了
② are on sale　正在打折特賣
③ have been discontinued　已經停產了

> 注意，on sale 指「打折特賣」，而 for sale 則是「待售」的意思，因此 It's not for sale. 不是指沒有折扣，而是非賣品的意思。

隨堂測驗 A

請依 CD 所播放的內容，完成下列對話。

Track 42

試試這樣說～   牛刀小試！

1 A: 我對你們的產品有一些問題。
   B: 好的，先生，請問是哪一項產品？

A: _____
B: Sure. Which product would that be, sir?

2 A: 如果您還有其他任何問題，請**隨時跟我們聯繫**。
   B: 好，謝謝。

A: Please _____
   if you have any more questions.
B: OK, thank you.

3 A: 感謝你的**迅速回覆**。
   B: 不客氣。

A: Thank you for your _____.
B: You're welcome.

4 A: KT 電腦您好。**您需要什麼協助嗎**？
   B: 你好，我想購買 K-100 型號的印表機。
   A: 噢，很抱歉，您詢問的產品**目前沒貨**。

A: KT Computers. _____
B: Hello, I'd like to buy the K-100 model printer.
A: Oh, I'm sorry. The product you inquired about is _____.

5 A: 可以請你寄一份**廣告冊**給我嗎？
   B: 沒問題。請問您的大名和地址。

A: Would you send me a _____, please?
B: Sure. Please give me your name and address.

隨堂
測驗

請聽 CD 完成下列三組不同情境的對話。

🔊 **Track 43**

1 你對型錄上看到的衣服很感興趣，請試著打電話去問問吧！

A: 布魯明黛兒百貨公司，您好。

B: 你好，我想問幾個關於你們一件商品的問題。

A: 好的。小姐，**請問是哪一個商品**？

B: 嗯，是有關一件胸罩。

A: 好的，那麼我幫您轉接到女性服飾部。

A: Hello, Bloomingdale's.

B: Hi, I have some questions about one of your products.

A: Sure. _____, ma'am?

B: Emm, it's about a bra.

A: OK, then I'll put you through to our women's apparel department.

🔊 **Track 44**

2 你接到找業務部負責人的來電，但是該位同仁今天請假，請試著將電話轉到客服部。

A: 喂，我是 IBM 的休修維。能不能請業務部人員聽電話？

B: **可以請問您有什麼事嗎**？

A: 我想詢問貴公司的一項產品。

B: 好的，不過我們所有的業務今天都休假。**我幫您轉接支援櫃台**。

A: 不用了，謝謝。我明天再打來。

B: 好的，**感謝來電**。

A: Hello, this is Hugh Hewitt calling from IBM. Could I speak to a sales representative, please?

B: _____

A: Yes, I'd like to inquire about one of your products.

B: OK. But all of our sales representatives are off today. Instead, _____

_____

A: No, thank you. I'll just call back tomorrow.

B: OK. _____

Track 45

3 你接到打來詢問商品是否有折扣的電話，請試著轉接業務部。

A: 您好，我是莉莉彼得森。您需要什麼協助嗎？

B: 我想問關於你們幾項產品的問題。

A: **謝謝您的詢問**。請問您的問題是？

B: **我想知道有沒有什麼折扣**？

A: 了解。**這樣的話，您需要與業務部聯繫**。

B: 好。請問你有他們的電話號碼嗎？

A: 我為您轉接。

B: 謝謝。

A: Hello, this is Lily Peterson. How may I help you?

B: Yes, I have some questions about a few of your products.

A: _____

What would you like to know?

B: _____

A: I see. _____

B: Right. Do you have their number?

A: I'll put you through.

B: Thank you.

Answers

隨堂測驗 A

1 I have some questions about your product.　　2 feel free [don't hesitate] to contact us
3 quick response [answer]　　4 (How) May I help you? / sold out right now　　5 brochure

隨堂測驗 B

1 Which product would that be
2 May I ask what this is concerning? / I'll put you through to the help desk. / Thank you for calling.
3 Thank you for your inquiry. / I'd like to know about any possible discounts. / In that case, you should contact the sales department.

2

下單與接單

How can I order this?

〉〉請跟著 Kevin 一起練習用英語打電話處理訂單。

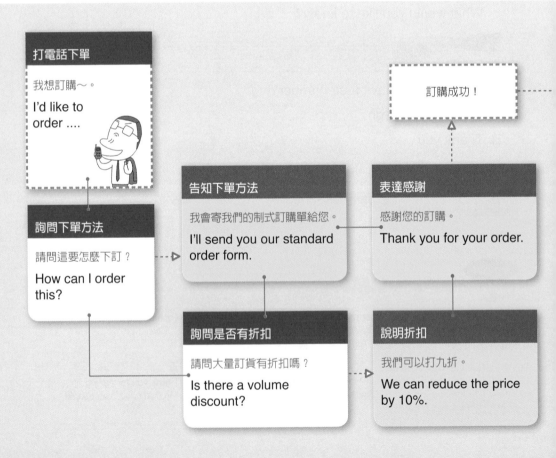

打電話下單

我想訂購～。

I'd like to order ....

詢問下單方法

請問這要怎麼下訂？

How can I order this?

告知下單方法

我會寄我們的制式訂購單給您。

I'll send you our standard order form.

詢問是否有折扣

請問大量訂貨有折扣嗎？

Is there a volume discount?

表達感謝

感謝您的訂購。

Thank you for your order.

說明折扣

我們可以打九折。

We can reduce the price by 10%.

訂購成功！

Kate 老師的重點提示

◆ 訂單 **order (n.)** 除了訂單之外，還有「秩序、指示」等意思，因此要透過文章脈絡來確定涵義。

◆ 下訂單 **place an order** order 一字作動詞時即可表示「下訂單」之意，不過若將 order 當名詞，前面加上 place 作動詞來使用的話，語感較為正式。

◆ 訂單確認 **order confirmation** 確認預約、訂位或訂單時就用 confirm（動詞）或 confirmation（名詞）這個字。

◆ 訂單狀態 **order status** status 是「地位、狀態」的意思，可以用這個字來詢問訂單的處理進度與出貨狀況。

◆ 接受訂單 **take an order** 動詞用 take 這個字。順帶一提，Can I take your order?「要點菜了嗎？」也是常見用法。

◆ 訂購單 **order form/sheet** 如果是公司與公司間的交易，為了避免誤解與錯誤，通常會使用記載品項與數量等內容的正式表單。

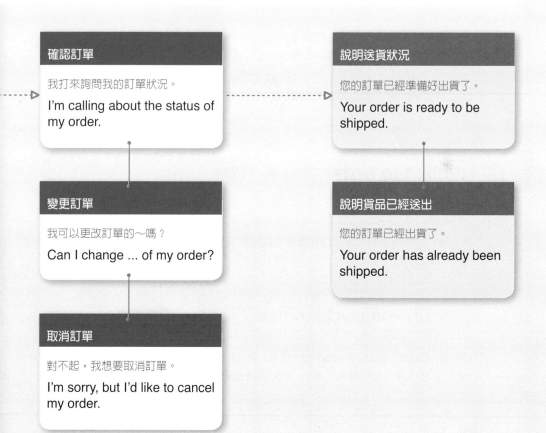

確認訂單

我打來詢問我的訂單狀況。

I'm calling about the status of my order.

變更訂單

我可以更改訂單的～嗎？

Can I change ... of my order?

取消訂單

對不起，我想要取消訂單。

I'm sorry, but I'd like to cancel my order.

說明送貨狀況

您的訂單已經準備好出貨了。

Your order is ready to be shipped.

說明貨品已經送出

您的訂單已經出貨了。

Your order has already been shipped.

🔵 Track 46

How can I order this?

請問這要怎麼下訂？

本句的 order 是動詞，若要改以片語 place an order 表達，就說 How can I place an order for this (product)?。

A How can I order this printer?
請問要怎樣訂購這台印表機？

B You can give me the product number as listed in the catalog.
請告訴我型錄上列的產品編號。

I'd like to order two A-100s.

我想訂兩台 A-100s。

也可以說 I'd like to place an order for two A-100s.。若要表達「我想要～」，比起 I want to ... ，I'd like to ... 較委婉，一般商務應用會使用此句型。當要取消訂單時，則可說 I'd like to cancel my order, please.（我想取消訂單）。

A I'd like to order two A-100s.
我想訂兩台 A-100s。

B Could you please send us your order by fax or email?
可以請您透過傳真或 email 將訂單傳給我們嗎？

Thank you for your order.
感謝您的訂購。

Thank you for placing your order with us. 或 Thank you for your business.（感謝您與我們交易），也都是相當適宜的說法。

> A I placed an order yesterday. When can I expect the delivery?
> 我昨天下了一張訂單。請問什麼時候會收到貨？
>
> B Thank you for your order, Mrs. Andrew. It should be delivered in two to three days.
> 感謝您的訂購，安德魯女士。應該兩到三天就會送到。

I'm calling about the status of my order.
我打來詢問我的訂單狀況。

查詢訂單時這句話就很好用。或者也可以說 I'd like to check the status of my order.（我想確認一下我訂單的狀況）。

> A Hello, I'm calling about the status of my order.
> 喂，我打來詢問我的訂單狀態。
>
> B Sure. What's your order number?
> 好的。請問您的訂單編號？

Your order is ready to be shipped.
您的訂單已經準備好出貨了。

ship 最常用的意思是「船」，但是作動詞使用時則是「運送、寄送」的意思，而且不一定是用船運，基本上可以用來表達所有運送方法。而網路購物常見的「免運費」，則可說 / 寫成 free shipping。

· Your order has already been shipped.
　您的訂單已經出貨了。

· Your order was shipped yesterday, so you'll probably get it today or tomorrow.
　您的訂單昨天已經出貨，所以您應該會在今明兩天收到。

06 Can I change the quantity of my order?
我可以更改訂單的數量嗎？

「訂貨量」就是 quantity of the order。注意，quality 是指「品質」，不要搞混了。

- Can I change the color of the shirt I ordered?
  可以更改我訂的襯衫顏色嗎？
- Is there a way to change one of the items that I ordered?
  可以更改我訂單裡的一個品項嗎？

07 I'll send you our standard order form.
我會寄我們的制式訂購單給您。

「格式、表格」為 form，「填寫表格」為 fill out (the form)。注意，不要因為是要填空格就誤用成 fill "in"。

A Mr. Stevens, we'll send you our standard order form. You can just fill it out and send it back to us.
史蒂文思先生，我會傳制式訂單給您，填完之後請回傳。

B OK. I appreciate your help.
好的，感謝您的協助。

08 You can pay COD.
您可以貨到付款。

COD 是 Collect On Delivery 或 Cash On Delivery 的縮寫，也就是「貨到付款」之意。而超商取貨付款則可說 / 寫成 pick up and pay for your package at the convenience store。

A If you don't want to pay by credit card, you can also opt to pay COD.
如果您不想刷卡結帳，也可以選擇貨到付款。

B That sounds good.
聽起來很不錯。

We have a minimum order requirement.

我們有最低數量限制。

當客戶的訂單數量太少時就可以這樣說。相反地，最高數量則為 maximum。

A We have a minimum order requirement for free shipping. You must order at least three items. Sorry for the inconvenience.
要免運費我們有最低的數量限制。您至少需要訂三件。抱歉造成您的困擾。

B That's OK. I guess I'll order three then.
沒關係。那我就訂三件吧。

Is there a volume discount?

請問大量訂貨有折扣嗎？

這個問題是在問折扣條件 (discount term)。有些公司可能會提供某些折扣，因此下單時可以先問 What are your discount terms?（貴公司的折扣條件是什麼？）。volume discount 指購買一定數量以上時會提供的折扣。

· We offer a 10% discount for cash purchases.
用現金支付的話打九折。

· We can reduce the price by 15% if you order one hundred or more.
如果您訂購一百個以上的話打八五折。

🎵 **Track 47**

「折扣」不是 D/C！

筆者曾看過有人將「折扣」縮寫成 D/C，這是不正確的！記得，折扣的英文就是 discount。

· We'll give you a 20% discount if you buy today.
今日購買打八折。

· That's the largest discount we can give you.
這是我們能提供的最大折扣。

請確實開口反覆練習，讓自己熟悉這些句型。　　🔊**Track 48**

我想～。

I'd like to _____.

① place an order　下單
② check the status of my order　查詢訂單
③ cancel my order　取消訂單

如果想要接電話者直接幫你確認訂單時，可以說
I'd like you to check the status of my order.。

可以更改～嗎？

Can I change _____?

① the quantity of my order　訂單數量
② the color of the shirt　襯衫顏色
③ the shipping method　運送方式

運送方式有 standard delivery（標準配送）、expedited
delivery（快遞）、next-day delivery（隔日送達）、
same-day delivery（當日送達）等。

 隨堂測驗 A 請依 CD 所播放的內容，完成下列對話。

🔴 Track 49

試試這樣說～   牛刀小試！

1 A: 我想**查詢訂單狀況**。
B: 好的。請問您的訂單編號是？

A: I'd like to _____.
B: Sure. What is the order number?

2 A: 我想要下單。
B: 謝謝您。**請線上稍等**。

A: I'd like to place an order.
B: Thank you. _____

3 A: 所以，貨九號會到嗎？
B: 是的，如果到時候您沒有收到，請**儘管聯繫我們**。

A: So, is the shipment going to arrive on the 9th?
B: Yes. Please _____
if you don't receive it by then.

4 A: 首次訂貨的顧客有**最低訂貨量限制**。
B: 噢，了解。請問是多少個？

A: We have a _____
for first time customers.
B: Oh, I see. What is it?

5 A: 請問有**大量訂貨折扣**嗎？
B: 有的。如果您訂超過五十個的話，我們會打七五折。

A: Is there a _____?
B: Sure. We can give you a 25% discount
if you order fifty or more.

請聽 CD 完成下列三組不同情境的對話。

🎧**Track 50**

1　請試著打電話給辦公用品公司訂購產品編號 2310 的名片盒。

A: 您好，這裡是藍丘辦公用品公司。您需要什麼協助嗎？

B: **我想要下單。**

A: 好的。請問您要訂購什麼產品？

B: 名片盒，**產品編號 2310**。

A: 好的，請稍等一下。

A: Hello, this is Blue Hill Office Supplies. Can I help you?

B: _____

A: OK. Which product would you like to order?

B: The business card package. _____

A: OK, please hold on just a second.

🎧**Track 51**

2　有客戶來電要變更訂單內容，但是商品已經出貨了。

A: 你好，我打來想問一下我的訂單。請問可以更改內容嗎？

B: 當然可以。**請問您的訂單編號幾號？**

A: 42A-52B。

B: 很抱歉，簡金斯先生，**您的訂單已經出貨了。**

A: 噢，我知道了。謝謝你撥出時間。

A: Hello. I'm calling about my order. Can I change it?

B: Sure. _____

A: It's 42A-52B.

B: I'm sorry, Mr. Jenkins, _____.

A: Oh, I see. Well, thank you for your time.

⊙Track 52

3 客戶打來想要確認訂單狀況，而貨品大概兩到三天之後會到。

A: **我打來想問一下訂單的狀況。**

B: 好的，請問您的訂單編號是？

A: 86P2。

B: 很抱歉，因為假日的關係我們出貨有點延遲。您的訂單應該會在明天出貨。

A: 了解。**請問貨什麼時候會到？**

B: 配送大概要兩到三天左右。

A: 謝謝。

A: _____

B: OK, may I have the order number?

A: It's 86P2.

B: I'm sorry, but we're experiencing some delay in shipment because of the holidays. Your order should go out tomorrow.

A: I see. _____

B: It should take about two to three days.

A: Thank you.

Answers

隨堂測驗 A

1 check the status of my order   2 Please hold on just a minute.   3 don't hesitate to contact us
4 minimum order requirement   5 volume discount

隨堂測驗 B

1 I'd like to place an order, please. / The product number is 2310.
2 What's your order number? / but your order has already been shipped
3 I'm calling about the status of my order. / When can I expect delivery?

Week

2

提出與處理客訴

I haven't received my order yet.

| 星期日第二堂課 |

》》請跟著 Kevin 一起練習關於客訴既專業又實用的句子。

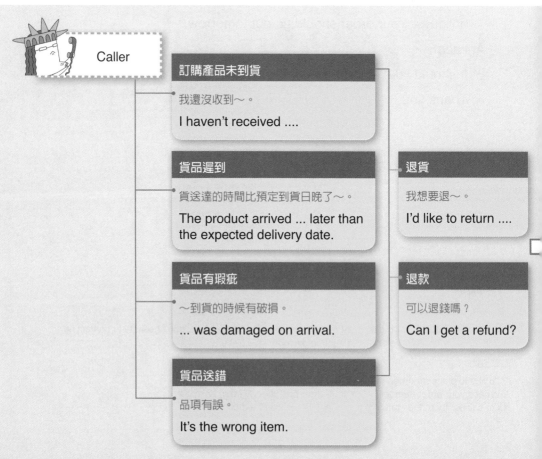

Caller

訂購產品未到貨

我還沒收到～。

I haven't received ....

貨品遲到

貨送達的時間比預定到貨日晚了～。

The product arrived ... later than the expected delivery date.

貨品有瑕疵

～到貨的時候有破損。

... was damaged on arrival.

貨品送錯

品項有誤。

It's the wrong item.

退貨

我想要退～。

I'd like to return ....

退款

可以退錢嗎？

Can I get a refund?

Kate 老師的重點提示

◆ 客訴 **complaint (n.)** 表達客訴的動詞要用 make。

◆ 提出客訴 **complain about** complain 是「對～表示不滿」的意思，通常和 about 一起使用。注意，complain 字尾加上 t 就變成名詞。

◆ 送貨 **shipment / delivery (n.)** ship 的動詞指「運送」，運送的「貨品」就叫 shipment。

◆ 延遲 **delay (n./v.)**「運送延遲」即 delay in shipping。

◆ 比預定日程晚 **behind schedule** behind 除了指「之後」外也可指「晚於」。

◆ 預計到貨 **be scheduled to arrive** arrive 本身是「抵達」的意思。

Responder

道歉

這件事我很抱歉。

I'm sorry about that.

保證改善

這種狀況不會再發生。

That won't happen again.

退款處理

我們會全額退款給您。

We'll give you a full refund.

提供抵用金

我們會提供您商店購物抵用金。

We'll give you store credit.

是……

當訂購的貨品無故晚到、破損或送錯時，就用下列這些句子來提出客訴；同時，也學習如何慎重、有禮貌地處理客訴電話。

🔊 **Track 53**

I haven't received my order yet.
我還沒收到我訂的貨。

也可用 My order hasn't arrived yet. 來表達。

A I haven't received my order yet.
我還沒收到我訂的貨。

B Oh, really? When did you place your order?
噢，真的嗎？請問您是什麼時候下單的？

The shipment has been delayed.
出貨延遲了。

收到訂單卻無法立即送貨時可利用此句先告知客戶，而若能加上原因則更佳。說明原因時可利用 due to 或 because of 這兩個片語，雖然 due to 語氣較硬，但是也更為正式。

A The shipment has been delayed due to computer problems.
出貨因電腦問題而有些延遲。

B OK, then when can you ship it?
好，那你們什麼時候可以出貨？

The product was damaged during shipment.
貨品在運送途中受損了。

也可以說 The product is defective.（這批貨有瑕疵品）。而如果是說 The product was already damaged upon arrival.，則是指「貨到就發現產品有破損」。

A The product was damaged during shipment.
貨品在運送途中受損了。

B I'm so sorry about that. If you send the item back, we will gladly replace it free of charge.
非常抱歉。麻煩請將貨寄回來，我們會很樂意地免費換貨給您。

It's the wrong item.
品項有誤。

即送錯貨的意思。也可以說 I got the delivery, but it's not what I ordered.（貨我收到了，但並不是我訂的東西）。順帶一提，This is not what I ordered. 這句話在餐廳裡也很常用。

A Hello. I got a delivery from you, but it's the wrong item.
你好。我收到你們送來的東西，但是品項有誤。

B Oh, sorry. Can I have your order number, please?
噢，抱歉。請問您的訂單編號幾號？

I'd like to return an item.
我想退貨。

return 除了有「回去」的意思之外，也可以用來表示「把物品送回去」。

A I'd like to return an item.
我想退貨。

B OK. Is there something wrong with it?
好的。請問產品有什麼問題嗎？

Can I get a refund?
可以退錢嗎 ？

「退款」叫 refund，如「退稅」就說成 tax refund。另外，跟公司申請餐費或出差費的「退款」則用 reimbursement 這個單字。

A Can I get a refund for this?
   這個產品我可以退費嗎 ？

B Sure. Just bring it in with the receipt.
   可以。請把它和收據一起帶過來就可以了。

We'll give you store credit.
我們會提供您商店購物抵用金。

當無法退費但可以用其他產品交換時就請這樣說。store credit 一般就是可於商家當作現金使用的點數或抵扣券等不同形式的證明。

· Mr. Locke, we are not able to give you a cash refund because you don't have the receipt. But we'll give you store credit.
  洛克先生，因為您沒有收據我們沒辦法以現金退款給您，但是我們可以提供您購物抵用金。

The product arrived four days later than the expected delivery date.
貨送達的時間比預定到貨日晚了四天。

或者簡單地說 The product arrived four days late. 也 OK。

A The product arrived four days later than the expected delivery date.
   貨送達的時間比預定到貨日晚了四天。

B I'm sorry about that. It happens during the holidays.
   很抱歉，假期的時候就會這樣。

This won't happen again.

這種狀況不會再發生。

客戶因各種狀況表示不滿時就用這個句子來跟客戶道歉。

A We apologize for the delay. This won't happen again.
很抱歉延遲了。這種狀況不會再發生。

B Thank you. If it does happen again, I'm going to have to change distributors.
謝謝。如果再發生的話,我就要換經銷商了。

We'll give you a full refund.

我們會全額退款給您。

在國外退錢或換貨是很容易的,甚至只是對產品不滿意都可以帶著產品回去要求退費。

A I bought one of your scales from your website but it's not as sturdy as I thought it would be.
我在你們網站上買了一個體重計,但是它沒有我想像中的堅固。

B OK, ma'am, just send it back to us and we will give you a full refund.
好的,女士,請寄還給我們,我們會全額退款給您。

🔊Track 54

網路購物

顧名思義,網路購物就是 Internet/online shopping。網路商家的頁面上通常都設有顧客(不)滿意度留言板,或留有客服電話。若要客訴,可參考下列說法。

· You sent me the wrong item. 你們寄來的品項不對。
· The clothes smell old. I'd like to get a refund, please.
衣服有舊舊的味道,我想要退錢。
· It's much smaller than I expected. 東西比我預期的小很多。

請確實開口反覆練習，讓自己熟悉這些句型。　　　　　　⏺Track 55

我訂的貨～。

The product I ordered _____.

① hasn't been delivered yet　還沒有送到
② isn't the one I received　不是我收到的
③ was damaged when I opened it　打開時發現是破損的

This isn't what I ordered. / I received the wrong product.
這兩種說法也都能表達「送錯產品」。

我什麼時候可以～？

When can I _____?

① get the product delivered　收到貨品
② expect to get a refund　收到退款
③ receive a replacement　收到退換的貨

通常收到的貨有破損或故障時廠商會用同樣的新品來
更換，而此時這個替換品就叫作 replacement。

OK?

隨堂測驗 A

請依 CD 所播放的內容，完成下列對話。

Track 56

試試這樣說～

牛刀小試！

1 A: 我打來問我訂的貨。我還沒有收到。
B: 好的。**您是何時下訂單？**

A: I'm calling about an order I placed. I haven't received it yet.

B: I see. _____

2 A: 我訂了兩個，但是**只收到一個**。
B: 好的，請告訴我您的訂單編號，**我幫您確認。**

A: I ordered two, but _____.

B: OK, if you give me your order number,

_____

3 A: 我收到貨品的時間比**預定到貨日**晚。
B: 噢，很抱歉，可能是因為假期的緣故。

A: I received the shipment later than the

_____.

B: Oh, sorry. It's probably because of the holiday season.

4 A: 我們會寄**替換品**給您。
B: 噢，謝謝。我需要把**破損的**寄回去嗎？

A: We will send you a _____.

B: Oh, thank you. Do you want me to send the _____ back to you?

5 A: 我可以退款嗎？
B: **您有收據嗎？**

A: Can I get a refund for this?

B: _____

🔊Track 57

1 四天前訂的貨還沒到，請試著打電話去客訴。

A: 早安您好，這裡是格林廣場。

B: 你好，**我訂了貨但是還沒有收到**。

A: 請問您什麼時候下的訂單？

B: **四天前**。我訂了一些文具用品。

A: 文具用品通常隔天就會到貨。我幫您查一下。

A: Good morning, this is Green Plaza.

B: Hi, _____

A: Oh, when did you place the order?

B: _____ I ordered some office supplies.

A: Office supplies are normally next-day delivery. Let me check.

🔊Track 58

2 顧客打電話來抱怨收到的產品有破損，請確認訂單內容之後表示會協助換貨。

A: 你好，我跟你們訂了一個產品剛剛收到，但是產品損壞得很嚴重。

B: 噢，真的嗎？**請問您貴姓大名？**

A: 我叫麥修貝利。

B: 好的。您訂的是瑪麗蓮夢露的畫，對嗎？

A: 對，玻璃是破的，我拆包裝的時候相框也是破損的。

B: 真是非常抱歉。**我們會立刻寄替換品給您。**

A: Hello, I ordered a product from you, and it was just delivered. But it's severely damaged.

B: Oh, really? _____

A: It's Matthew Bailey.

B: OK. You ordered the portrait of Marilyn Monroe, correct?

A: Yes, the glass was broken, and the frame was damaged when I opened it.

B: I am so sorry about that. _____

⊙Track 59

3　你收到錯誤的產品，請試著打電話給賣方客訴。

A: 客服中心您好，我是瑞克。請問您需要什麼協助？

B: 你好，我是辛蒂康納。**我打來問我訂的貨。**

A: 您收到了嗎？

B: 收到了，但**不是我訂的產品**。

A: 噢，真的很抱歉。

B: **我可以退錢嗎**？

A: 我們會免費寄正確的品項給您。送錯的您可以留著。

B: 聽起來很不錯，謝謝。

A: Customer Service, Rick speaking. How may I help you?

B: Hello. This is Cindy Conners. _____

A: Did you receive it?

B: Yes, but _____ .

A: Oh no. I'm sorry about that.

B: _____

A: We'll send you the correct item for free. And you can keep the wrong item.

B: That sounds good. Thank you.

Answers

隨堂測驗 A

1 When did you place the order?　2 I only got one / I'll verify the order.　3 expected delivery date
4 replacement / damaged one　5 Do you have the receipt?

隨堂測驗 B

1 I placed an order but haven't received it yet. / Four days ago.
2 May I have your name? / We'll send you a replacement right away.
3 I'm calling about my order. / it's the wrong item / Can I get a refund?

A. 請利用括弧內的提示填空以完成句子。　　　　　　　　　　　　🔊**Track 60**

1 A: 一起吃個午餐討論一下吧。

B: 好啊。**你哪一天方便**？(What day / good)

A: Why don't we discuss this over lunch?

B: Sure. _____

2 A: 感謝您來電吉爾伯企業。請問您需要什麼協助？

B: 你好，**我想問幾個關於你們產品的問題**。(questions / product)

A: Thank you for calling the Gilbert Corporation. How may I help you?

B: Hi. _____

3 A: **要怎麼訂購你們型錄上的產品**？(order / from your catalog)

B: 您跟我說產品編號就可以了。

A: _____

B: You can just give me the product number.

4 A: **我還沒有收到我訂的貨品**。(receive / order)

B: 噢，真的嗎？請問您的訂單編號是？

A: _____

B: Oh, really? What's the order number?

5 A: **我星期四整天都有空**。(free all day)

B: 噢，那我星期四去你辦公室找你。

A: _____

B: Oh, then I'll visit you at your office on Thursday.

B. 請將下列對話中文部分翻譯成英文。

🔘**Track 61**

A: Hello, is Mr. Estvander there?

B: Speaking.

A: Oh, hi. This is Sue from Liberty Management. I'm calling about the order you recently placed with us.

B: Is there a problem?

A: No. ① 我是要跟你說因為電腦出了問題，出貨有一些延遲。

B: I see. ② 那你們什麼時候可以出貨？

A: We will be able to ship it tomorrow. ③ 非常抱歉延遲了。

B: That's all right. Thank you for calling.

A: You're welcome. Have a good day, sir.

Ans.

① _____

② _____   ③ _____

🔘**Track 62**

A: Tommy Jackson.

B: Hello, Tommy. This is Mary. I'm calling about our meeting on Monday.
　④ 很抱歉，我得取消我們的會面。我們能改期嗎？

A: Oh, OK. ⑤ 那妳哪一天方便？

B: How about Tuesday?

A: OK, what time?

B: One or two in the afternoon?

A: ⑥ 我下午不行。 Do you think you can come in the morning?

B: Yes, I can probably get there around 10:45. Is that OK?

Ans.

④ _____

⑤ _____   ⑥ _____

C. 請和 Kate 老師一起模擬接打電話，做雙向問答練習。

＊ 本單元錄音內容共有兩遍，第一遍的每一句之間保留了較長的間隔，請利用空檔做跟讀練習；練習完之後，請再聽一遍正常語速的版本。

🎵Track 63

接聽電話

請扮演 Kevin 的角色，練習接 Kate 的電話。

Kevin：感謝您來電蓋吉公司，我是林建文。請問您需要什麼協助？

Kate：Hi, I have some questions about your products. Is there a number I can call?

Kevin：您可以撥打電話找我們的客服中心人員談談，電話是 555-3333。

Kate：Thank you. Can I call the number now?

Kevin：可以。我們的客服中心全年無休，服務時間是從早上九點到下午六點。

Kate：OK. Thank you.

🎵Track 64

接聽電話

請扮演 Kevin 的角色，練習接 Kate 的電話。

Kevin：布魯斯公仔玩偶店您好。

Kate：Hi, I've placed an order online, but I'm going to have to cancel it, please.

Kevin：好的。請告訴我您的訂單編號。

Kate：Sure. It's BB4PEG.

Kevin：您的訂單已經取消完成。可以請教您取消的原因嗎？

Kate：Oh, it's because I forgot I already had the product.

* 全篇對話之中文翻譯請左右兩頁對照參閱。

撥打電話

接下來換你練習打電話給 Kate。

Kate : Thank you for calling Gadgets Company. My name is Kate Kim. How can I help you?

Kevin : 喂，我想問幾個關於貴公司產品的問題。請問我要打幾號？

Kate : You can talk to one of our customer service representatives. The number is 555-3333.

Kevin : 謝謝。請問可以現在打嗎？

Kate : Yes. The Customer Center is open seven days a week, from 9 a.m. to 6 p.m.

Kevin : 好的，謝謝。

撥打電話

請再練習打電話給 Kate。

Kate : Hello. Bruce's Hobby Shop.

Kevin : 妳好，我在網路上下了一個訂單，但是我想取消。

Kate : OK. Can I have your order number?

Kevin : 好，編號是 BB4PEG。

Kate : Your order's canceled. Can I ask why you wanted to cancel it?

Kevin : 噢，因為我忘記我已經有那個產品了。

複習時間 Answers

A

1 What day would be good for you?
2 I have some questions about your products.
3 How can I order a product from your catalog?
4 I haven't received my order yet.
5 I'm free all day Thursday.

B

① I wanted to let you know that the shipment has been delayed because of a computer problem.
② When can you ship it then?
③ I am so sorry about the delay.
④ I'm sorry but I have to cancel it. Can we reschedule?
⑤ What day would be good for you then?
⑥ I'm not available in the afternoon.

翻譯

下單
A: 您好，請問艾斯班德先生在嗎？
B: 我就是。
A: 您好，我是自由管理公司的蘇，我是為了您最近下的訂單來的。
B: 有什麼問題嗎？
A: 沒有，我是要跟您說因為電腦出了問題，出貨有一些延遲。
B: 我知道了。那你們什麼時候可以出貨？
A: 我們明天就可以出貨。非常抱歉延遲了。
B: 沒關係。感謝妳打電話來。
A: 不客氣。祝您有個愉快的一天。

約定會面
A: 我是湯米傑克森。
B: 湯米你好，我是瑪麗，我打來說一下我們週一會議的事情。很抱歉，我得取消我們的會面。我們能改期嗎？
A: 噢，好。那妳哪一天方便？
B: 星期二如何？
A: OK，幾點？
B: 下午一兩點如何？
A: 我下午不行。妳早上可以過來嗎？
B: 好，我大概十點四十五分可以到。這樣好嗎？

3

Week

商務篇②

打錯電話

What number did you dial?

>> 請跟著 Kevin 一起練習如何用英語應對打錯電話的狀況。

有人打錯電話

請問這是～辦公室嗎？

Is this ... office?

確認欲通話對象

請問您找哪位？

Who are you looking for?

表明欲通話對象

我找～。

I'm looking for ....

確認電話號碼

請問您打的是幾號？

What number did you dial?

確認電話號碼

這裡不是 736-2013 嗎？

Isn't this 736-2013?

Kate 老師的重點提示

◆ 撥打 **dial (v.)** dial 原指「撥打數字盤」，在電話皆已換成按鍵式之後，英語仍使用此單字。

◆ 打錯 **dial the wrong number** 也可說成 have the wrong number。

◆ 找 **look for** 電話中要「找～」時就使用此片語。

◆ 電話號碼無誤 **the number is right** 雖然查無此人但對方打的電話號碼「沒有錯」時就這樣說。例如：「這裡沒有這個人，但是號碼是對的。」即 There's nobody by that name here, but the number is right.。

◆ 恐怕～ **I'm afraid ...** 此句型帶有「很抱歉 / 很遺憾～」的語感。

◆ 寫下號碼 **write the number down** write something down 即「寫下～」之意，而 I must have written the number wrong. 就是在說「我一定是記下錯誤的號碼了」。

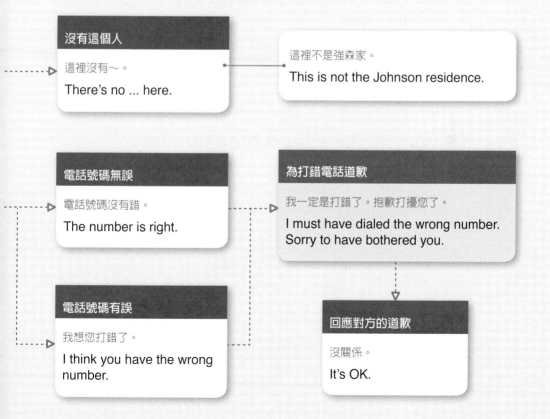

沒有這個人

這裡沒有～。

There's no ... here.

這裡不是強森家。

This is not the Johnson residence.

電話號碼無誤

電話號碼沒有錯。

The number is right.

為打錯電話道歉

我一定是打錯了。抱歉打擾您了。

I must have dialed the wrong number.
Sorry to have bothered you.

電話號碼有誤

我想您打錯了。

I think you have the wrong number.

回應對方的道歉

沒關係。

It's OK.

任何時候都可能會有意外狀況發生，打電話時也是一樣。接到有人打錯電話，或是自己不小心打電話時該怎麼辦？首先不要慌張，用幾句簡單的英語就能有禮貌地應對。

🎧 Track 65

What number did you dial?

請問您打的是幾號？

當你覺得對方打錯電話時就可以這樣說，也可以用 call 來替換 dial。如果在前面加上 I'm sorry, but ... 就能使句子聽起來更為莊重有禮。

A I'm sorry, but what number did you dial?
不好意思，請問您打的是幾號？

B Oh, isn't this 311-0864?
噢，這裡不是 311-0864 嗎？

I think you have the wrong number.

我想您打錯了。

wrong number 是 wrong telephone number 的簡略，也可以說 I'm afraid you have the wrong number. 或 I'm afraid you called the wrong number.。

A I think you have the wrong number.
我想您打錯了。

B Oh, I'm sorry.
噢，很抱歉。

Isn't this 213-4161?

這裡不是 213-4161 嗎?

注意,在英語裡接電話的那方須用 this 表達,不是 that,也不是 there。

> A Isn't this 213-4161?
> 這裡不是 213-4161 嗎?
>
> B Oh, it's 213-6141.
> 噢,是 213-6141。

The number is right.

電話號碼沒有錯。

當要表達「您撥的電話號碼沒錯」的時候就可以這樣說,也可替換成 The number you have is right. 或 You have the right number.。

> A Is this Ms. Banks' office?
> 這是班克斯小姐的辦公室嗎?
>
> B I'm afraid you called the wrong number.
> 您恐怕打錯電話了。
>
> A Isn't this 555-2345?
> 這裡不是 555-2345 嗎?
>
> B The number is right, but there's no Ms. Banks here.
> 電話號碼沒有錯,但是這裡沒有班克斯小姐。

Who are you looking for?

請問您找哪位?

詢問來電者所找的對象是誰時就這麼說,而另一方面,「我找~」就是 I'm looking for ....。

> A Who are you looking for?
> 您找哪位?
>
> B I'm looking for Mr. Harry Winston. Isn't this 224-6810?
> 我找哈利溫斯頓先生。這裡不是 224-6810 嗎?

There's nobody here by that name.

這裡沒有叫這個名字的人。

此句型的重點在於介系詞須用 by。

A Isn't this 820-2224? I'm looking for Ms. Yoona Huang.
那裡不是 820-2224 嗎？我找黃允兒小姐。

B The number's right, but there's nobody here by that name.
號碼沒有錯，但是這裡沒有叫這個名字的人。

There's no John here.

這裡沒有約翰這個人。

若要表達「電話號碼沒有錯，但是沒有那個人」，也可以這麼說。

A The number you have is right. But there's no John here.
您打的電話號碼沒有錯，但是這裡沒有約翰這個人。

B OK. Sorry to bother you.
好的。抱歉打擾您了。

This is not the Johnson residence.

這裡不是強森家。

the Johnson residence 指「強森一家住的地方」，即「強森家」，而 the Johnson's residence 則是正式的說法。

A You got the right number, but this is not the Johnson residence.
你的電話號碼沒有錯，但是這裡不是強森家。

B OK. Sorry to bother you.
好的。抱歉打擾您了。

I must have dialed the wrong number.
我一定是打錯了。

當自己打錯電話時，這句話就能派上用場。類似的表達方式還有 I must have the wrong number. ，或者可以說 I must have written the number down wrong.（我一定是記下錯的號碼了）。

A I must have dialed the wrong number. I'm sorry.
　　我一定是打錯了。抱歉。

B That's OK. Bye.
　　沒關係，再見。

Sorry to have bothered you.
抱歉打擾您了。

打錯電話表示歉意時也可以簡單地說 I'm sorry. 就好，不過如果像主題句一樣說成 Sorry to bother you. 或 I'm sorry to have bothered you. ，則更有禮貌。

A I must have dialed the wrong number. Sorry to have bothered you.
　　我一定是打錯了，抱歉打擾您了。

B That's all right! Bye.
　　沒關係！再見。

🔊**Track 66**

沒關係
接受道歉時，除了最常見的 That's all right.、That's OK. 之外，下列幾種說法也很道地。

· No problem. 沒有問題。
· Don't worry about it. 別放心上。
· That's cool. 沒關係。（年輕人常用的說法）

請確實開口反覆練習，讓自己熟悉這些句型。　**Track 67**

我想～。

I think ⬛⬛⬛⬛⬛⬛.

① you have/got the wrong number　你打錯了
② I must have dialed the wrong number　我一定是打錯了
③ you wrote/copied the number down wrong　你記下錯誤的號碼了

> 「記下」的說法有
> [write / put / copy] something down 等。

這裡不是～嗎？

Isn't this ⬛⬛⬛⬛⬛⬛⬛?

① 234-5678　234-5678
② Ms. Haley Blunt's residence　海莉布朗家
③ Derek Computer　德瑞克電腦

> 用英語唸電話號碼時和中文一樣，一個數字一個數字唸就好。美
> 國的電話號碼通常是七位數，前面再加上區域號碼 (area code)。
> 例如 (312) 922-8567（芝加哥）、(808) 672-5490（夏威夷）等。

隨堂測驗 A

請依 CD 所播放的內容，完成下列對話。

🔘**Track 68**

試試這樣說～

牛刀小試！

1 A: 喂，**我找格瑞佩克先生**。
B: 抱歉，這裡沒有格瑞這個人。

A: Hello. _____ Mr. Gregory Peck.

B: I'm sorry. There's no Gregory here.

2 A: **請問您打的是幾號？**
B: 123-4567。

A: _____

B: 123-4567.

3 A: 我想**你記下錯誤的號碼了**。
B: 噢，抱歉。

A: I think _____.

B: Oh, sorry.

4 A: 瑞塔在嗎？
B: 噢，我想**你打錯了**。

A: Is Rita there?

B: Oh, I think _____.

5 A: 您恐怕是打錯了。
B: 噢，**抱歉打擾您了**。

A: I'm afraid you have the wrong number.

B: Oh, _____.

111

請聽 CD 完成下列三組不同情境的對話。

🔴Track 69

1 有人打電話來找可翠娜高伯，但是這裡沒有這個人。

A: 喂，可以請可翠娜高伯小姐聽電話嗎？
B: **抱歉，這裡沒有人叫那個名字。**我想您一定是打錯了。
A: 這裡不是 890-1234 嗎？
B: 是沒有錯。**你說你要找誰？**
A: 高伯小姐⋯⋯噢，對不起，我給錯名字了。我是要找可翠娜格林頓小姐。

A: Hello, may I speak to Ms. Katrina Goldberg?

B: _____

I think you must have the wrong number.

A: Isn't this 890-1234?

B: Yes, that's right. _____

A: Ms. Goldberg ... Oh, I'm sorry. I gave you the wrong name. It's Ms.
Katrina Gellington.

🔴Track 70

2 有人打電話來找格雷，但是應該是打錯了。

A: 喂，可以請格雷聽電話嗎？
B: **這裡沒有格雷這個人。**
A: 真的嗎？這裡不是 532-1125 嗎？
B: **抱歉，您一定是打錯了。**
A: 噢，抱歉打擾您了。
B: 沒關係。

A: Hello, may I speak to Grey?

B: _____

A: Really? Isn't this 532-1125?

B: _____

A: Oops. Sorry to have bothered you.

B: _____

🔊Track 71

3　你打電話給湯姆畢斯曼但是撥錯了區域號碼。鄭重地向對方道歉吧。

A: 喂，我是西斯蓋普。可以請湯姆畢斯曼先生聽電話嗎？

B: 抱歉，這裡沒有人叫那個名字。請問您打的是幾號？

A: 678-9990。

B: 嗯……奇怪了，號碼沒有錯。

A: **區域號碼是 555，沒錯吧？**

B: 噢，不，這裡是 565。

A: **抱歉打擾您了。**

A: Hello, this is Seascape. Can I talk to Mr. Tom Peaceman?

B: I'm sorry. There is no one here by that name. What number did you dial?

A: 678-9990.

B: Hmm. That's strange. The number's right.

A: _____

B: Oh, no. It's 565 here.

A: OK, _____

Answers

Week 3

答錄機語音

Please leave your name and number.

| 星期六第二堂課 |

>> 請跟著 Kevin 一起練習如何用英語錄製語音訊息。

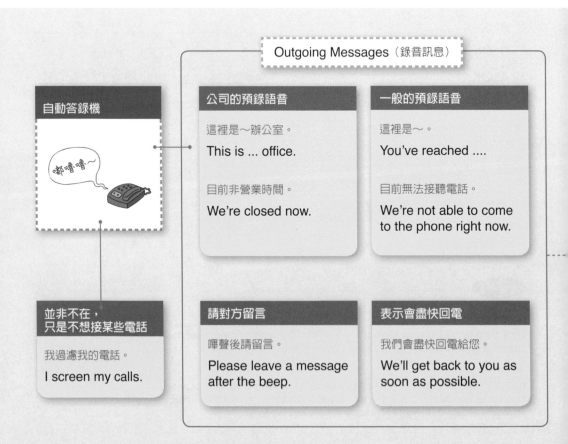

Outgoing Messages（錄音訊息）

自動答錄機

嘟嚕嚕～

公司的預錄語音

這裡是～辦公室。
This is ... office.

目前非營業時間。
We're closed now.

一般的預錄語音

這裡是～。
You've reached ....

目前無法接聽電話。
We're not able to come to the phone right now.

並非不在，只是不想接某些電話

我過濾我的電話。
I screen my calls.

請對方留言

嗶聲後請留言。
Please leave a message after the beep.

表示會盡快回電

我們會盡快回電給您。
We'll get back to you as soon as possible.

Kate 老師的重點提示

◆ 電話答錄機 **answering machine** 不要認為是「自動」的應答系統就直覺要用 automatic 這個字。

◆ 留言 **leave a message** 雖然是在機器上錄音,但是不能講成 record a message。

◆ 嗶聲 **the beep** beep 是「嗶聲」的狀聲詞。

◆ 無法接聽 **away (from the phone)** 指因為人不在所以沒辦法接電話,也可以說 not able to come to the phone。

◆ 回電 **return a phone call** 聽到留言後回撥電話給來電者。

◆ 語音訊息 **outgoing/incoming message** 在公司或家裡的答錄機裡留下的「現在不在」等訊息叫作 outgoing message,簡稱 OGM;打電話來的人在答錄機裡留下的訊息則為 incoming message,簡稱 ICM。

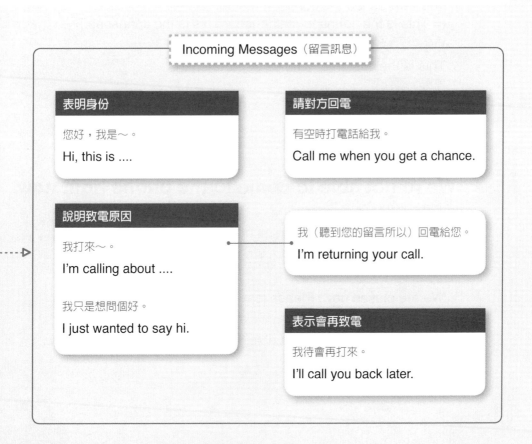

Incoming Messages(留言訊息)

表明身份

您好,我是～。
Hi, this is ....

說明致電原因

我打來～。
I'm calling about ....

我只是想問個好。
I just wanted to say hi.

請對方回電

有空時打電話給我。
Call me when you get a chance.

我(聽到您的留言所以)回電給您。
I'm returning your call.

表示會再致電

我待會再打來。
I'll call you back later.

電話英語通關句 TOP 10

本堂課要教各位的是如何錄製公司歡迎語音，以及電話答錄機或手機語音信箱的留言和回應說法。

Please～ leave your message

🎵 **Track 72**

You've reached the Johnsons.
這裡是強森家。

這是錄製電話答錄機訊息起頭時最常用的句型，表示「你現在是打電話到了～家」。講「～的家」時要在姓氏後面加上 s，比方說 the Johnsons、the Chens。

- You've reached the Johnson residence.
  (= This is the Johnson residence. / This is the Johnsons.)
  這裡是強森家。

- This is the customer service department.
  這裡是客服部。

- This is 335-2412.
  這裡是 335-2412。

We're not able to come to the phone right now.
目前無法接聽電話。

You've reached ... 後面通常會接這句話，如果想要表達「不在」，也可以說 We're away from the phone.。不過就算不在家，一般在電話錄音也不會說 I'm not home right now.（我現在不在家）。

- We are closed now. Please leave a message.
  目前非營業時間，請留言。

- My husband and I are not able to come to the phone right now.
  我與我先生此刻無法接聽電話。

Please leave a message after the beep.

嗶聲後請留言。

這個句子除了在電話轉到手機的語音信箱時會聽到之外，也常用在電話答錄機的 OGM (outgoing message) 上。after the beep 就是「嗶聲響之後」，也可以說 after the tone。

- After the tone, please leave a message.
  請在嗶聲後留言。

- Please leave a message after the beep and I'll get right back to you.
  嗶聲後請留言，我會盡快回電給您。

Please leave your name and number.

請留下您的姓名與電話號碼。

在聽到留言之後有時會需要回電，因此通常也會請對方留下電話號碼。另外，如果想請對方留下簡單的訊息，就用 a short message 替換。

- Please leave your name, number, and a short message.
  請留下您的姓名、電話和簡短訊息。

- If you leave your name and number, I'll return your call as soon as possible.
  如果您留下姓名和電話號碼，我會盡快回電給您。

I'll get back to you as soon as I can.

我會盡快回電給你。

get back to 即「再打電話給～」之意。除了 as soon as I can 之外，也可以說 as soon as possible。另外，as soon as possible 可縮寫為 ASAP。

- Please leave a message. We'll get back to you as soon as we can.
  請留言，我們會盡快回電給您。

- Michael, will you please get back to me ASAP?
  麥可，可以請你盡快回電給我嗎？

Let the machine get it.

讓答錄機接吧。

當下不想接電話，或者看到不想接的電話時就可以這樣說。此狀況和故意不接手機讓來電轉到語音信箱是一樣的意思。

A Isn't that your phone ringing?
你的手機是不是在響？

B Oh. Just let the machine get it.
噢，就讓機器接吧。

I screen my calls.

我過濾我的電話。

如果是有來電者顯示 (caller ID) 功能的電話可輕易地過濾來電，不然就是使用電話答錄機，並透過對方留下的語音訊息來判斷是否要接聽，此即為 screen (my) calls。

A Your phone's ringing. Aren't you going to pick it up?
你的電話在響，你不接嗎？

B I screen my calls. I'm going to see who's calling first.
我在過濾電話，先看看是誰打來的再說。

I'm just calling to say hello.

我只是打來問個好。

下列也是用於表達致電目的之常見說法。

· I just wanted to say hi.
我只是想問個好。

· I'm calling to see if you can come to my party on Friday.
我打來問你週五可不可以來我的派對。

I'm returning your call.

我（聽到您的留言所以）回電給您。

不管是透過答錄機或手機語音信箱得知對方曾來電，或者看到未接來電顯示而回電，這句話都能派上用場。

A Hello, my name is John David. I'm returning your call.
喂，我是約翰大衛，回電給您。

B Yes, this is Tina at Golden Chinese Restaurant. I called you about your reservation tomorrow.
是的，我是高登中菜館的婷娜，我打來確認您明天的訂位。

Call me when you get a chance.

有空時打電話給我。

若說 Call me when you get this message. ，則為「聽到訊息之後請回電給我」的意思。when you get a chance 也可用於請對方回 email。例如 Drop me a line when you get a chance.（有空時請回信）。

- Hi, this is Melissa. It's 10:30 in the morning on Tuesday. I just wanted to say hi. Call me when you get a chance! Bye.
嗨，我是梅莉莎。現在是星期二早上十點半，我只是打來問聲好。有空時回個電話給我！掰。

🔊 Track 73

留言戳記

手機語音信箱大都會告知留言的日期與時間，但是電話答錄機則不一定有這樣的功能，因此留言時最好也一併錄下。

- It's Wednesday, August 22nd, about 4:30.
現在是八月二十二號星期三下午四點半左右。

核心句型練習

請確實開口反覆練習，讓自己熟悉這些句型。 🎧 **Track 74**

我只是打來～。

I'm just calling to _____.

① say hi/hello　問個好
② see if we can have diner together tomorrow　看我們明天晚上能不能一起吃個飯
③ see if we can meet next week　看我們下禮拜能不能碰個面

> 要表達「想問是否～」時用 ask if 當然也可以，但是 see if 有「想知道是否～」的感覺，聽起來更自然。

請～打電話給我。

Please give me a call _____.

① as soon as possible　盡快
② when you get a chance　有空時
③ tomorrow morning　明天早上

> 「打電話給我」可直接說 call me，但在日常生活中 give me a call 也時常聽到。

隨堂測驗 A

請依 CD 所播放的內容，完成下列對話。

🔊 **Track 75**

 試試這樣說～

 牛刀小試！

1 您好，**這裡是凱特辦公室**。我現在沒有辦法接聽電話，**請留言**，我會盡快回電。

Hello. _____

I'm not able to come to the phone right now,

so _____,

and I'll get back to you as soon as I can.

2 您好，我是馬克。**嗶聲後**請留下您的**姓名與電話**，我會盡快回電。謝謝。

Hello, this is Mark. Please leave your

_____

and I'll get back to you as soon as possible.

Thank you.

3 感謝來電 KT 電子。我們的**營業時間**是週一到週五，上午八點到下午五點。請留下簡短訊息，我們會**盡快**回電給您。

Thank you for calling KT Electronics. Our

_____ are Monday through

Friday, from 8 a.m. to 5 p.m. Please leave

a short message, and we'll get back to you

_____.

4 這裡是史都華家。我們此刻**無法接聽電話**，請在嗶聲後留言。

You've reached the Stewart _____.

We're _____

right now, so please leave a message after

the tone.

🔊 **Track 76**

1 如果有不想接的電話，過濾電話是一個好方法。

A: **你的電話在響**。你不接嗎？

B: **噢，就讓機器接吧**。

A: 為什麼 ?

B: **我在過濾電話**。我接到一大堆白痴電話。

A: 電話推銷員打來的嗎？

B: 一點都沒錯。幾乎每天。

A: 原來如此。

A: _____ You're not going to get it?

B: Oh, _____.

A: Why?

B: _____ I get a lot of stupid phone calls.

A: From telemarketers?

B: Exactly. Almost every day.

A: I see.

🔊 **Track 77**

2 請試著錄製公司的自動語音訊息 (OGM)。

感謝您來電 KT 電信公司。目前非營業時間。

我們的營業時間是週一至週五，早上九點到晚上六點。

請留言。**我們會盡快回電。**

_____   _____

Our business hours are Monday through Friday, from 9 a.m. to 6 p.m.

Please leave a message. _____

Track 78

3   你打電話去史提芬家但是沒有人接。請試著在自動答錄機上留言。

A: 嗨，這裡是史提芬家。我們此刻無法接聽電話，請留下您的姓名與電話，我們會盡快回電，謝謝。

B: 嗨，我是克里斯。**我打來看你們星期五能不能來參加我女兒麗莎的生日派對。**晚上六點在我們家。**請回個電話給我！**

A: Hi, you've reached the Stevens residence. We're not able to come to the phone right now. Please leave your name and number, and we'll get back to you as soon as we can. Thank you.

B: Hi, this is Chris. _____

_____

It's at my place at six o'clock. _____

Week

3

| 星期日第一堂課 |

國際電話

I'd like to place a collect call.

〉〉請跟著 Kevin 一起練習如何用英語應對國際電話。

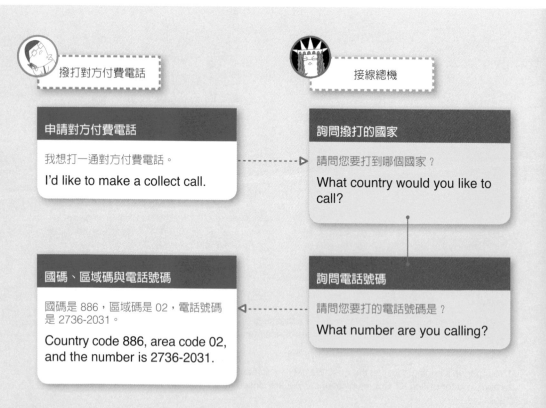

撥打對方付費電話

申請對方付費電話

我想打一通對方付費電話。

I'd like to make a collect call.

接線總機

詢問撥打的國家

請問您要打到哪個國家？

What country would you like to call?

國碼、區域碼與電話號碼

國碼是 886，區域碼是 02，電話號碼是 2736-2031。

Country code 886, area code 02, and the number is 2736-2031.

詢問電話號碼

請問您要打的電話號碼是？

What number are you calling?

Kate 老師的重點提示

◆ 國際電話 **international (phone) call** 另外，市內電話是 local (phone) call，長途電話是 long distance (phone) call。

◆ 對方付費電話 **collect call** 這種由接收者付費的電話有時是透過接線總機接通，或者撥打一個專用的號碼來連接。而「撥打對方付費電話」即 place/make a collect call。

◆ 接線總機；接線生 **operator (n.)** 負責連接對方付費電話的人，他們會先與接收者通話確認對方是否願意接聽。

◆ 電話卡 **calling card** 國際電話卡則為 international (phone calling) card。

◆ 井字鍵 **(#) the pound key** 用電話卡打國際電話時會聽到 Please press/enter your phone number followed by the pound key. 這樣的語音，意思是「電話號碼輸入完畢後請按井字鍵」。順帶一提，米字鍵 (*) 的英文是 the star key。

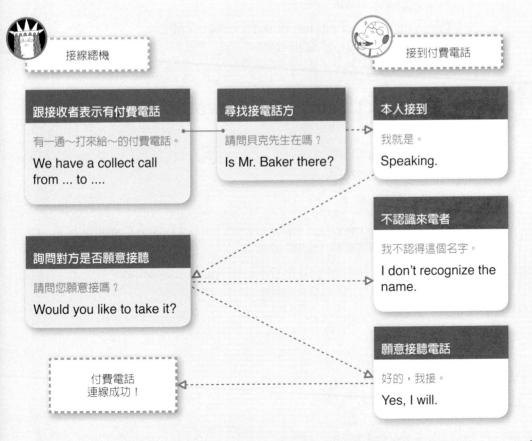

電話英語通關句 TOP

到國外出差、旅遊時常會需要打國際電話。本週我們主要要學的不是打電話，而是撥打對方付費電話時會用到的表達方式，以及與國際電話費用相關的內容。

🔊 **Track 79**

I'd like to place a collect call.
我想打一通對方付費電話。

接通總機之後首先先說這一句。「撥打電話」的動詞除了 place 之外，也可以 make 替換：make a phone call。

· I want to make a collect call to Paris.
  我想打一通對方付費電話到巴黎。

· Can you please help me make a collect call?
  可不可以麻煩幫我打一通對方付費電話？

I'll connect you to the operator.
我幫您轉接總機。

打電話去電信公司要求撥打對方付費電話時會聽到這句話。接著只要說出國碼、區域碼和欲撥打的電話號碼就 OK。

> A I'd like to make an international collect call to Canada.
>   我想打一通國際對方付費電話去加拿大。
>
> B OK, I'll connect you to the international operator.
>   好的，我幫您轉接國際接線總機。

Would you like to take a collect call?

您願意接收一通付費電話嗎？

接線總機會問接收者願不願意接聽須由接受方付費的電話，此時通常也會告知來電者的
所在地與姓名。

A You have a collect call from Amber Chang from Malaysia. Would you like to take it?
您有一通張安珀從馬來西亞打來的對方付費電話。請問您願意接嗎？

B Yes, I will.
好的，我接。

I don't recognize the name.

我不認得這個名字。

注意，這種情況要用 recognize 這個字。

A Would you like to take a collect call from Ms. Amy Harris?
您願意接一通由艾咪哈利斯小姐打來的對方付費電話嗎？

B Amy Harris? I don't recognize the name.
艾咪哈利斯？我不認識這個人。

I'd like to sign up for the international calling service.

我想申請國際電話服務。

有時候跟電信公司申請國際電話服務時還可獲得折扣，特別是美國國內長途電話的費用
相當高，因此會用很多方法吸引顧客。

A I'd like to sign up for the international calling service.
我想申請國際電話服務。

B OK. May I have your phone number, please?
好的。請問您的電話幾號？

International calls are cheaper at night.

打國際電話夜間較便宜。

國際電話和手機通訊有時在晚上或週末會比較便宜，甚至有夜間某個時段免費的狀況。

A International calls are cheaper at night.
國際電話晚上打比較便宜。

B Really? By how much?
真的嗎？便宜多少？

I'd like to get a calling card.

我想買一張電話卡。

電話卡就是一種預付卡的概念，講多少就從餘額扣除多少。

A I'd like to get an international calling card.
我想買一張國際電話卡。

B Which country are you going to call the most?
請問您主要是打到哪一個國家？

What kinds of international calling plans do you have?

你們有什麼樣的國際電話方案？

這是針對電信公司問的問題。plan「計畫」，在此則是「資費方案」的意思，比方說 long distance plan「長途電話方案」等。

A What kinds of international calling plans do you have?
你們有什麼樣的國際電話方案？

B We have a "nickel nation" plan. You can call anywhere in the world, and it's a nickel a minute.
我們有一個「五分國」方案，全世界不管打去哪裡都是一分鐘五分錢（1 nickel = 5 cents）。

Please enter the country code and area code followed by the phone number.

請輸入國碼和區域碼，再輸入電話號碼。

無論使用國際電話方案或預付卡，都會聽到這樣的語音指示。國碼就是每個國家的固定號碼。

- Please enter the country code and area code followed by the phone number.
  請輸入國碼和區域碼，再輸入電話號碼。

  ～輸入之後～

- Please wait while we connect your call.
  轉接中，請稍候。

You have 31 minutes left on your card.

您的電話卡還有三十一分鐘通話時間。

國際電話卡通常是預付性質，可通話時間會隨著使用而減少。本句是在通話前告知剩餘時間的訊息。

- Please enter the card number.
  請輸入卡號。

- You have 10 minutes left on your card.
  您的電話卡還有十分鐘通話時間。

🔵Track 80

卡號

國際電話卡上通常都印有卡號，輸入卡號之後就會有訊息告知剩餘使用時間。購入電話卡時，只要將被遮蓋住的地方刮掉 (scratch off) 即可看見卡號。有些國際電話卡還附有加值功能，而「加值」的英文就是 recharge。

A: I'd like to get this card recharged, please.　我想加值這張卡。
B: How much?　加多少？
A: $20, please.　二十美元。
B: Here you go. This will give you about 100 minutes.
　好了。您大概可以再通話一百分鐘。

請確實開口反覆練習，讓自己熟悉這些句型。　🎧**Track 81**

我想～。

I'd like to _____.

① make an international call to France　打一通國際電話去法國
② place a collect call　打一通對方付費電話
③ get an international calling card　買一張國際電話卡

> 在美國若要打長途電話，一般會跟電信公司申請長途電話服務以獲得優惠折扣；要不然就是使用電話卡。假如使用一般家用電話打長途電話的話，費用相當高。

～多少錢？

How much _____?

① is an international phone call to Japan　打一通到日本的國際電話
② is this international calling card　這張國際電話卡
③ is your international calling plan per minute　你們的國際電話方案每分鐘

> 預付卡的英文叫作 prepaid card。字首 pre- 指「～之前的」。舉例來說，preschool 就是「學前」的意思。

隨堂測驗 A

請依 CD 所播放的內容，完成下列對話。

🎧 Track 82

 試試這樣説～

 牛刀小試！

1 A: 您好，這裡是 AT&T。您有一通從美國傑克森先生打來的**對方付費電話**。**請問您願意接嗎**？
　　B: 好的，我接。

A: Hello. This is AT&T. You have a
_____ Mr. Jackson
from the United States. _____
_____

B: Yes, I will.

2 A: 您好，我想打一通對方付費電話到澳洲。
　　B: 請問**您要打的電話號碼是**？

A: Hello, I'd like to make a collect call to
Australia, please.

B: _____
_____, please?

3 A: 感謝您來電史普林特。
　　B: 我想**打一通對方付費電話到**英國。

A: Thank you for calling Sprint.

B: Yes, I'd like to _____
_____ the U.K.

4 A: 從美國打到韓國要**多少錢**？
　　B: **每分鐘**十分錢。

A: _____
to call Korea from the United States?

B: It's ten cents _____.

5 A: 你們有什麼樣的**國際電話方案**？
　　B: 我們有一個「夜間免費」方案。

A: What kinds of _____
_____ do you have?

B: We have a "night free" plan.

131

🔵 Track 83

1   請試著打電話去太平洋電信公司申請一通打回台灣的對方付費電話。

A: 感謝您來電太平洋電信公司。**您需要什麼協助嗎？**

B: **我想打一通對方付費電話去台灣。**

A: 噢，好。我幫您轉接國際電話總機。

B: 謝謝。

～接通總機之後～

C: 請問您要打的電話是幾號？

A: Thank you for calling Pacific Telecom. _____

B: Yes. _____

A: Oh, sure. I'll connect you to the international operator.

B: Thank you.

   (operator)

C: May I have the phone number you're calling, please?

🔵 Track 84

2   接線總機說你有從湯姆瑞德打來的對方付費電話，請試著回答。

A: 喂？

B: 您好，我是中華電信的接線總機。**您有一通從湯姆瑞德打來的對方付費電話。請問您願意接嗎？**

A: 湯姆瑞德？

B: 他說他是您的表弟。

A: 噢，是的。**我願意接。**請幫我接通。

A: Hello?

B: Hello. This is the operator from Chunghwa Telecom. _____

_____

A: Tom Reed?

B: He says he's your cousin.

A: Oh, right. _____ You can connect us.

🔊**Track 85**

3　你需要打國際電話到韓國和日本。請試著詢問個別的國際電話費然後購入預付卡。

A: **你們有什麼樣的國際電話方案？**

B: 您要打到哪個國家？

A: 韓國和日本。

B: 好的。韓國是每分鐘十分錢，日本是每分鐘十八分錢。

A: 了解。**你們有賣預付卡嗎？**

B: 有的。我們有五十元和一百元的。

A: **我要一張五十元的，麻煩你。**

A: _____

B: What country will you be calling?

A: Korea and Japan.

B: OK. Korea is 10 cents a minute, and Japan is 18 cents a minute.

A: I see. _____

B: Yes. We have 50-dollar ones and 100-dollar ones.

A: _____

Answers

隨堂測驗 A

1 collect call from / Would you like to take it?　　2 May I have the number you're calling
3 make [place] a collect call to　　4 How much does it cost / per minute　　5 international calling plans

隨堂測驗 B

1 How can I help you? / I'd like to make a collect call to Taiwan, please.
2 Would you like to take a collect call from Mr. Tom Reed? / I'll take it.
3 What kinds of international calling plans do you have? / Do you sell prepaid calling cards? / I'd like to get a 50-dollar one, please.

收訊不良、手機沒電等狀況

I can't talk right now.

〉〉請跟著 Kevin 一起練習應對關於電話有可能發生的狀況。

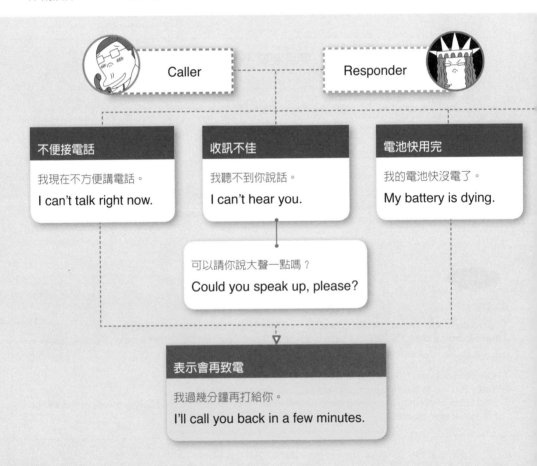

Caller

Responder

不便接電話

我現在不方便講電話。

I can't talk right now.

收訊不佳

我聽不到你說話。

I can't hear you.

電池快用完

我的電池快沒電了。

My battery is dying.

可以請你說大聲一點嗎？

Could you speak up, please?

表示會再致電

我過幾分鐘再打給你。

I'll call you back in a few minutes.

Kate 老師的重點提示

◆ 打擾 **interrupt (v.)** 對方不方便接電話但需要與他通話時最好先說一句「抱歉打擾你」，也就是 Sorry to interrupt you.。另外，打斷對方說話時也可以這樣說。

◆ 雜訊；雜音 **noise (n.)**

◆ 成片斷 **break up** 本片語除了最常聽到的「與戀人分手」的意思之外，當電話中一下聽到一下聽不到，可以用 You're breaking up. 傳達「聽不清楚你說什麼，斷斷續續的」之意。

◆ 線路干擾 **cross (v.)** 通訊受到干擾就是 The lines are crossed.。

◆ 連結（狀況）**connection (n.)** 如果聽到電話一直傳來雜音，就可以說 This is a bad connection.（通話品質很差）。

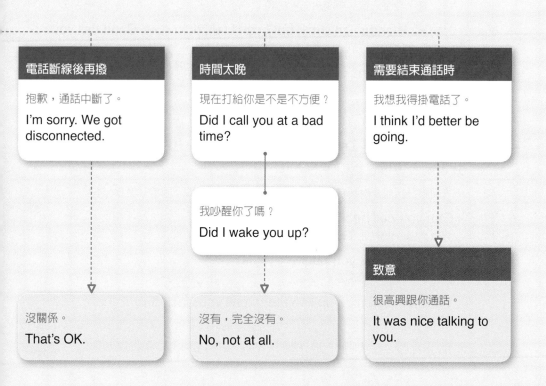

電話斷線後再撥

抱歉，通話中斷了。
I'm sorry. We got disconnected.

時間太晚

現在打給你是不是不方便？
Did I call you at a bad time?

我吵醒你了嗎？
Did I wake you up?

需要結束通話時

我想我得掛電話了。
I think I'd better be going.

致意

很高興跟你通話。
It was nice talking to you.

沒關係。
That's OK.

沒有，完全沒有。
No, not at all.

電話英語通關句 TOP 10

重要會議上突然電話響了，此時須向對方表達「現在不太方便」的話，英文要怎麼說？或是聽不清楚對方的聲音，還是電池快沒電了⋯⋯諸如此類的狀況，該如何用英語應對？

🎧 Track 86

I can't talk right now.
我現在不方便講電話。

或者也可以說 It's not a good time to talk.。can't talk 原本是「不能說話」的意思，但是在電話上則為「無法接電話」之意。因此問對方「現在方便講電話嗎？」就會是 Can you talk right now?。

> A　Hello, this is Wanda. Is Mr. Chu there?
> 喂，我是汪達。請問朱先生在嗎？
>
> B　Hi, Wanda. I'm sorry, but I can't talk right now. Can I call you back?
> 嗨，汪達。抱歉我現在不方便講話，可以待會回電給妳嗎？

I'll call you back in a few minutes.
我過幾分鐘再打給你。

不方便講電話而要掛斷時就可以這樣說，而 call back 即「回電」之意。

- Can you call back later?
  可以請你待會再打來嗎？

- Is it OK if I call you back?
  我可以待會回電給你嗎？

- What time would you like me to call you back?
  你什麼時候方便我可以再打給你？

- Why don't you call me again when you get to your office?
  你何不等回到辦公室時再打給我？

I can't hear you.

我聽不到你說話。

當周圍太吵或通話品質不佳而聽不清楚對方聲音時就可以這樣說。

· I can barely hear you.
  我幾乎聽不到你說話。

· It's really loud.
  好吵。

· We have a bad connection.
  通訊品質不好。

Could you speak up, please?

可以請你說大聲一點嗎？

環境太吵或通話品質不良而聽不清楚對方說話時，不妨先試著找個安靜的地方，要不就請對方講大聲一點。沒聽到或要請對方再說一遍就是 What did you say? / Say that again?。

A I'm sorry, but I can't hear you because it's very loud here. Could you speak up, please?
抱歉，這邊好吵我聽不到你說話。可以請你說大聲一點嗎？

B OK. Where – are – you – now?
好。你～現～在～在～哪～裡？

A Oh, I still can't hear you. Let me go outside.
噢，還是聽不到。讓我出去說。

The reception here is terrible.

這裡的收訊很差。

拜科技進步之賜，現在利用手機通訊 APP 也能免費通話，只不過，有時容易遇到收訊不良的狀況導致無法順暢地講事情，這種時候就可以用這句話向對方解釋。

A The reception here is terrible.
這裡收訊好差。

B OK, let me call you back on your landline.
OK，我再打到你室內電話。

137

My battery is dying.
我的電池快沒電了。

有時候會因為手機沒電而中斷通話。英語中是用電池 is dying「快死掉」來形容這種狀況，或者也可以說 My battery is running out.。

A I'm sorry, but my battery is dying.
抱歉，我的電池快沒電了。

B Oh, OK. Do you want to call me back?
噢，好。那你要再打來嗎？

We got disconnected.
通話中斷了。

因為是「連結」的中斷，直接用 disconnect 這個單字就好。要讓對方知道不是故意掛斷，而是非預期的狀況。

A I guess we got disconnected. There must be a weak signal here or something.
剛剛電話斷了。也許是這裡訊號太弱或什麼的。

B That's OK. Actually I can come to your office right now, and we can talk there.
沒關係。其實我現在可以過去你辦公室，我們在那邊談吧。

Did I call you at a bad time?
現在打給你是不是不方便？

這句話跟 Can you talk right now? 是一樣的意思。

A Did I call you at a bad time?
現在會不會不方便？

B No, not at all. What's up?
不會，一點都不會。什麼事？

Did I wake you up?

我吵醒你了嗎？

除非是急事，不然半夜打電話是很失禮的！打電話到國外時要小心，如果沒有算好時差，就很有可能打擾到別人的睡眠。如果不是故意要半夜打電話，記得一定要致上「很抱歉吵醒你」之意。

A Did I wake you up? I'm sorry, what time is it there?
  我是不是吵醒你了？抱歉，那邊現在幾點？

B It's midnight, but I was awake. Is this an emergency?
  這邊是半夜，但是我還醒著。有什麼急事嗎？

I think I'd better be going.

我想我得掛電話了。

也可以說 I'd better get going.。想要掛電話但是對方還在繼續說時，這句話就能派上用場。

A I'm sorry, but I think I'd better be going.
  抱歉，我想我得掛了。

B OK, it was nice to talk to you.
  好，很高興跟你通電話。

🎧Track 87

很高興和你通電話

下列幾個句子都能幫助你表達「很高興跟你通話」、「很久沒聊了很開心」等心情，在要掛電話時特別適用。

· It was nice talking to you. 很高興跟你通話。
· It was good to hear your voice. 很高興聽到你的聲音。
· It's good to talk to you again. 很開心又跟你談話。
· It was good to hear from you. 很高興接到你的電話。

我～再打給你。
I'll call you back _____.

① in a few minutes　過幾分鐘
② when I get to my office　回到辦公室
③ when I have a better signal　訊號比較好的時候

> 訊號叫 signal，如果訊號較強，收訊 (reception) 就會比較好。

因為～我聽不到你說話。
I can't hear you because _____.

① it's too loud here　這裡太吵
② the connection isn't very good　通話品質不太好
③ I'm on the subway　我在地鐵上

> 地鐵就是 subway，「在地鐵上」則說 be on the subway。注意，如果是坐公車就不用 the 而是要用 a，例如 I'm on a bus.（我在公車上）。

 試試這樣說～

牛刀小試！

Track 89

1 A: 您好，這裡是 AK 保險。請問游先生在嗎？

B: 我就是。抱歉，**我幾乎聽不到你說話，因為這邊很吵。**

A: Hello, this is AK Insurance. Is Mr. Yu there?

B: This is he. I'm sorry, but _____.

2 A: 您好，這裡是每日財經。請問蘇太太**在嗎？**

B: **我就是。**抱歉，我現在不方便講電話。**可以請你十五分鐘之後再打來嗎？**

A: Hello, this is *Business Daily*. Is Mrs. Su _____?

B: _____ I'm sorry, but I can't talk right now. _____

3 A: 我是 MCI 的林建文。可以請提普太太聽電話嗎？

B: 嗨，林先生。**我正在開會。**可以等我開完會再回電給您嗎？**大概半個小時之後會結束。**

A: This is Kevin Lin from MCI. Can I talk to Mrs. Tipper?

B: Hi, Mr. Lin. _____ _____ Can I call you back after the meeting? _____

4 A: 嗯，我想**我得掛電話了。**

B: 好，很高興**聽到你的聲音。**

A: Well, I think _____.

B: OK. It was good to _____.

請聽 CD 完成下列三組不同情境的對話。

🔊**Track 90**

1 不方便講電話時卻有人打來,請告訴對方五分鐘後會回電。

A: 您好,我是偉德集團的喬米爾斯。請問方小姐在嗎?

B: 我就是。米爾斯先生,**很抱歉,我現在不方便講電話。**

A: 噢,好的。我待會再打來。

B: **或是我可以五分鐘之後打給你嗎?**

A: 好的,謝謝。

A: Hi, this is Joe Mills at Wade Group. Is Ms. Fang there?

B: Speaking. Mr. Mills, _____.

A: Oh, OK. I'll call you back later.

B: _____

A: Sure, thank you.

🔊**Track 91**

2 接了電話但是電池快沒電了!請對方諒解電話可能隨時會掛斷。

A: 喂?

B: 嗨,史密斯先生,我是茱莉。最近好嗎?

A: 我很好。噢……抱歉。可以請妳說快一點嗎?**我的手機快沒電了。**

B: 噢,不是什麼急事。**我明天再打給您。**

A: 好的,茱莉。**到時候再聊。**

A: Hello?

B: Hi, Mr. Smith. This is Julie. How are you doing?

A: I'm all right. Oh ... I'm sorry. Could you speak quickly, please?

_____

B: Oh, it's not urgent. _____

A: OK, Julie. _____

⊙Track 92

3　打電話給吳老師但是很吵。吳老師，可以請您說大聲一點嗎？

A: 喂，吳老師嗎？

B: 我是。請問你哪位？

A: 我是艾科企業的蘿拉。吳老師，**我聽不到您說話**。

B: 是的，這邊很吵。

A: 老師，**可以請您說大聲一點嗎**？

B: **等一下**。我去外面⋯⋯好多了，我現在聽到了。

A: 好。我是為了您昨天寄給我的報告打來⋯⋯

A: Hello, Mr. Wu?

B: Yes, who is this?

A: This is Laura from the Echo Corporation. Mr. Wu, _____.

B: Yes, it's very loud here.

A: Sir, _____?

B: _____ Let me go outside. ... That's better. Now I can hear you.

A: OK. I'm calling about the report you sent me yesterday ...

Answers

隨堂測驗 A

1 I can barely hear you because it's very loud here
2 available / Speaking. / Can you call back in about 15 minutes?
3 I'm in a meeting right now. / It should be over in about 30 minutes.　　4 I'd better go / hear your voice

隨堂測驗 B

1 I'm sorry, but I can't talk right now / Or can I call you in about five minutes?
2 My battery is dying. / I'll give you a call tomorrow. / Talk to you then.
3 I can't hear you / could you speak up, please / Hang on.

A. 請利用括弧內的提示填空以完成句子。　Track 93

1 A: 您打的是幾號？(What number / dial)

B: 555-2311。

A: _____

B: 555-2311.

2 A: 我此刻無法接聽電話，請留言。(come to the phone, leave a message)

B: 您好，我是泰美。

A: _____

B: Hi, this is Tammi.

3 A: 我想打一通對方付費電話。(place)

B: 好的，電話號碼幾號？

A: _____

B: OK. What's the number?

4 A: 抱歉，我聽不到你說話。(can't hear)

B: 噢，真的嗎？要不要我回撥給你？

A: _____

B: Oh, really? Do you want me to call you back?

5 A: 詹姆士在嗎？

B: 我想你打錯了。(wrong number)

A: Is James there?

B: _____

B. 請將下列對話中文部分翻譯成英文。

🔊**Track 94**

A: Hello, ① 我找福萊德羅培茲先生。

B: ② 請問您打的是幾號？

A: 555-5157.

B: That's strange. The number's right, but ③ 這裡沒有叫這個名字的人.

A: Really? Is this 555-5157?

B: Yes. Who did you say you were looking for?

A: Fred Lopez.

B: Sorry. There's no Fred here.

A: OK. ④ 抱歉打擾您。

Ans.

① _____ ② _____

③ _____ ④ _____

🔊**Track 95**

A: Hello?

B: Hello, Harry? This is Sally. ⑤ 你現在方便講話嗎？

A: Oh, I'm sorry, but I'm in a meeting. I'll call you back.

B: Call me around one o'clock then.

A: OK. ⑥ 可以給我你的電話號碼嗎？

B: Sure, it's 555-1666. ⑦ 如果我沒接的話，請留下語音訊息。

A: ⑧ 那我就一點打給你。

B: OK, bye.

Ans.

⑤ _____ ⑥ _____

⑦ _____ ⑧ _____

C. 請和 Kate 老師一起模擬接打電話，做雙向問答練習。

* 本單元錄音內容共有兩遍，第一遍的每一句之間保留了較長的間隔，請利用空檔做跟讀練習；練習
完之後，請再聽一遍正常語速的版本。

◎Track 96

接聽電話

請扮演總機的角色，練習接 Kate 的電話。

Operator ：感謝您來電全球企畫。您需要什麼協助嗎？

Kate ：I'd like to make an international call to Singapore, please.

Operator ：好的。您是要打對方付費電話嗎？

Kate ：Yes, please. The number is 65432123.

Operator ：好的。請問您貴姓大名？

Kate ：It's Kate Kim.

◎Track 97

撥打電話

請扮演 Kevin 的角色，試著打電話給 Kate。

Kevin ：喂，凱特嗎？我是建文。

Kate ：Hi. How are you doing, Kevin?

Kevin ：我很好。妳在哪裡？好吵喔。

Kate ：I'm at a subway station. Can you hear me OK?

Kevin ：斷斷續續的。讓我打給妳吧。

Kate ：What? What did you say? I can't hear you!

* 全篇對話之中文翻譯請左右兩頁對照參閱。

撥打電話

請扮演 Kevin 的角色，試著撥打對方付費電話到新加坡。

Operator : Thank you for calling Global Plan. How may I help you?
Kevin　　：我想打一通國際電話到新加坡。
Operator : OK. Would you like to make a collect call?
Kevin　　：是的，麻煩你。號碼是 65432123。
Operator : OK. Can I have your name, please?
Kevin　　：林建文。

接聽電話

再來請練習接 Kate 的電話。

Kate　 : Hello. Kevin? This is Kate.
Kevin : 嗨，妳好嗎，凱特？
Kate　 : I'm doing OK. Where are you? It's loud.
Kevin : 我在地鐵站裡。妳聽得到我說話嗎？
Kate　 : You're breaking up. Let me call you back.
Kevin : 什麼？妳說什麼？我聽不到！

A

1 What number did you dial?
2 I can't come to the phone right now. Please leave a message.
3 I'd like to place a collect call, please.
4 I'm sorry, but I can't hear you.
5 I think you have the wrong number.

B

① I'm looking for Mr. Fred Lopez.
② What number did you dial?
③ there's nobody here by that name
④ I'm sorry to have bothered you.
⑤ Have you got a minute to talk?
⑥ Can you give me your number?
⑦ If I don't answer, leave a voice message.
⑧ I'll call you back at one then.

翻譯

打錯電話
A: 喂你好，我找福萊德羅培茲先生。
B: 請問您打的是幾號？
A: 555-5157。
B: 奇怪，號碼沒有錯，但是這裡沒有叫這個名字的人。
A: 是嗎？這裡是 555-5157 嗎？
B: 是的，您剛說您要找誰？
A: 福萊德羅培茲。
B: 抱歉。這裡沒有福萊德這個人。
A: 好。抱歉打擾您。

不方便接電話
A: 喂。
B: 喂，哈利嗎？我是莎莉。你現在方便講話嗎？
A: 噢，很抱歉我在開會。我再打給妳。
B: 那你一點左右打給我吧。
A: 好。可以給我妳的電話號碼嗎？
B: 好，我的電話號碼是 555-1666。如果我沒接的話，請留下語音訊息。
A: 那我就一點打給妳。
B: OK，掰。

W e e k

4

生活篇

Week

4

| 星期六第一堂課 |

祝賀與慰問

I'm calling to congratulate you on your promotion.

>> 請跟著 Kevin 一起練習用英語和工作夥伴維繫關係。

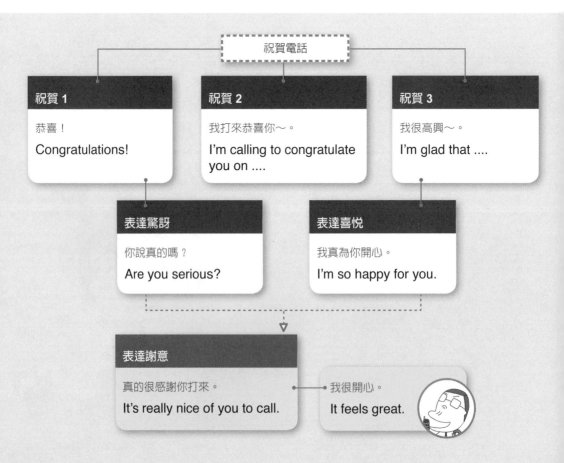

祝賀電話

祝賀 1

恭喜！

Congratulations!

祝賀 2

我打來恭喜你～。

I'm calling to congratulate you on ....

祝賀 3

我很高興～。

I'm glad that ....

表達驚訝

你說真的嗎？

Are you serious?

表達喜悅

我真為你開心。

I'm so happy for you.

表達謝意

真的很感謝你打來。

It's really nice of you to call.

我很開心。

It feels great.

Kate 老師的重點提示

◆ 祝賀 **congratulate (v.)**「祝賀～」就是 congratulate (someone) on (something)。

◆ 我聽說 **I heard ...** 如果是聽到消息或傳聞，只要簡單說 I heard ... 就好。

◆ 記得 **remember (v.)** 比方說要表達「謝謝你記得我的生日」，則為 Thank you for remembering my birthday.。

◆ 畢業 **graduation (n.)**「從～畢業」動詞 graduate 後面須加上介系詞 from。

◆ 通過考試 **pass the exam** 相反地，考試沒通過就叫 fail the exam。

◆ 恭喜你找到工作 **congratulations on (your) new job** 雖是同樣意思，不過 congratulations on getting a job 這種說法較少聽到。

◆ 晉升 **promotion (n.)** 除了指「晉升」之外，promotion 還有「宣傳、促銷」等意思，而「獲得晉升」即 get a promotion。

◆ 加薪 **raise (n.)**「獲得加薪」就是 get a raise。

慰問電話

慰問 1

好可惜～。

It's such a pity that ....

慰問 2

致上我最深的慰唁。

Please accept my deepest condolences.

慰問 3

很遺憾聽到～。

I was sorry to hear that ....

慰問 4

有什麼我可以幫上忙的地方嗎？

Is there anything I can do for you?

表示得到很大的力量

你不知道這對我的幫助有多大。

You don't know how much it helps.

電話英語通關句 TOP 10

職場上除了公事之外，偶爾也會有私事方面的交流，無論好事或壞事，適時地表達祝賀或慰問之意，以及適當地回應也都是很重要的。

---

01 I'm calling to congratulate you on your promotion.

我打來恭喜你晉升。

「為了 B 事祝賀 A」的句型為 congratulate A on B，介系詞用 on。

> A　Hello?
> 喂？
>
> B　Hello, Linda? This is Harry. I'm calling to congratulate you on your promotion.
> 喂，琳達嗎？我是哈利，我打來祝賀妳升官。

---

02 I'm so glad that you were chosen to lead the project.

我很高興你被選出來領導這個專案。

I'm glad (that) ... 用以表達對 that 後面的內容感到非常開心。

· I'm glad that you were promoted to director!
  我很高興你被升為處長了！

· I'm glad to hear that you got married!
  我很高興聽到你結婚了！

· I'm so happy to hear that you're feeling better now.
  我很高興聽到你現在感覺好多了。

A little bird told me you got a raise.

有人跟我說你加薪了。

A little bird told me ... 這種說法表示不清楚傳聞的出處，或者不想透露給對方知道是誰說的。當然也可以直接說 I heard you got a raise.。

A A little bird told me you got a raise. Congratulations!
有人跟我說你加薪了。恭喜！

B Oh, well, thank you. The walls have ears, I guess.
噢，嗯，謝謝。我想是隔牆有耳。

Congratulations on the new baby!

恭喜你生寶寶！

雖然是「孩子出生」，但是不需要用到 birth 這個字。on 後面可依所要祝賀的事情替換。

· Congratulations on your recovery!
恭喜你恢復健康！

· Congratulations on your graduation!
恭喜你畢業了！

· Congratulations on winning the election!
恭喜你贏得選舉！

· Congratulations on your new job!
恭喜你找到新工作！

I'm so happy for you.

我真為你開心。

這句可說是祝賀用的百搭句，舉凡是好事，一般都能適用。

A I heard you bought a new house! Congratulations! I'm really happy for you.
聽說你買了新房！恭喜！我真為你開心。

B Thank you. Why don't you come to our housewarming party?
謝謝。要不要來參加我們的新居派對？

Are you serious?

你說真的嗎？

serious 就是「認真」的意思。這句話可以用在好消息也可以用在壞消息上。另外，No way!（不可能！）或 I can't believe it!（我真不敢相信！）等也是常用的口語表達方式。

A　Did I wake you up? I'm sorry. But I had to tell you that I won the lottery!
　　我吵醒你了嗎？抱歉，但是我一定得告訴你我中樂透了！

B　Are you serious? Oh, my gosh! Congratulations!
　　你說真的嗎？噢，天啊！恭喜！

It's really nice of you to call.

真的很感謝你打來。

不管是喜事或令人傷心的事，都可以用這個句子來感謝對方的關心。

· Thank you for saying so.
　謝謝你這麼說。

· I'm really happy about the result.
　有這樣的結果我真的很開心。
　* happy for + 人 / happy about + 事

It feels great.

我很開心。

主詞也可用 I，說成 I feel great.。如果是 I feel good about myself.，則是因完成某件事而對自己感到驕傲的意思。

A　I heard your presentation was very successful. Congratulations!
　　聽說你的簡報很成功。恭喜！

B　Thank you! It feels great to finally achieve something.
　　謝謝！終於完成一件事的感覺真的很好。

It's such a pity that you had to cancel your vacation.

可用這句話來安慰他人，It's such a pity that ... 就是「～真是令人惋惜」的意思。

- I'm really sorry to hear that you didn't pass the exam.
  很遺憾聽說你考試沒有通過。

- Please accept my deepest condolences.
  致上我最深的慰唁。

- I was so shocked when I heard your son was in an accident.
  聽說你兒子發生意外我真的很震驚。

You don't know how much it helps.

你不知道這對我的幫助有多大。

當收到慰問電話時可以用這個句子來表達感謝。

A I just heard the tragic news. I'm so sorry.
   我剛聽說了這個壞消息，我很難過。

B Thank you for calling. You don't know how much it helps.
   謝謝你的來電。你不知道這對我有多大的幫助。

Track 99

太開心了！

下列句子用來表達喜悅或完成某事後感到內心充實都很貼切。

- It feels so good to have passed the test.
  通過考試感覺真是太棒了！

- I feel good about myself. It feels like I've done something.
  我為自己感到開心，感覺我終於完成了某事。

Week 4 | Sat.1

請確實開口反覆練習，讓自己熟悉這些句型。　🔊**Track 100**

我打來～。

I'm calling to ████████████ **.**

① congratulate you on your graduation　恭喜你畢業
② wish you a happy birthday　祝你生日快樂
③ say congratulations on your promotion　恭喜你獲得晉升

> 「晉升、升遷」可以用 get promoted 或 get a promotion 來表達，I got promoted! / I got a promotion! 都是「我升官了！」的意思。

我聽說你～！

I heard you ████████████ **!**

① got a (new) job　找到新工作了
② got a raise　加薪了
③ had a (new) baby　生了寶寶

> 美國有種習俗叫 "baby shower"，就是孕婦的親朋好友在生產前幫孕婦開的派對。另外，在結婚前幫新娘辦的派對則為 "bridal shower"。

OK?

隨堂測驗 A

請依 CD 所播放的內容，完成下列對話。

Track 101

試試這樣說～

牛刀小試！

1 A: 喂，我是安。**恭喜**你搬新家！
   B: 謝謝！找一天來玩。

A: Hello. This is Ann. _____
your new house!

B: Thank you! You should come visit sometime.

2 A: 喂，我是謝杰明。**聽說**你兒子找到一個不錯的工作。恭喜！
   B: 噢，謝先生，謝謝。

A: Hello, this is Jamie Hsieh. _____
your son got a good job. Congratulations!

B: Oh, Mr. Hsieh. Thank you.

3 A: 我**中樂透**了！
   B: **你說真的嗎**？恭喜！你中了多少？

A: I've _____!

B: _____
Congratulations! How much did you win?

4 A: 你猜怎麼著？這週末我要舉行我第一次的獨奏會！
   B: **恭喜**！我可以去嗎？

A: Guess what? I'm having my first recital this weekend!

B: _____ Can I go?

5 A: **很遺憾聽說**你太太發生了意外。
   B: 謝謝你的安慰。

A: _____ your
wife was in an accident.

B: Thank you for your kind words.

請聽 CD 完成下列三組不同情境的對話。

🎧 **Track 102**

1 請祝賀李先生獲得晉升。

A: 嗨，我是伊麗莎白。李先生在嗎？

B: 在，我就是。

A: 有人跟我說你升官了。我打電話來恭喜你。

B: 噢，謝謝妳。

A: Hi, this is Elizabeth. Is Mr. Lee there?

B: Yes, this is he.

A: _____

_____

B: Oh, thank you.

🎧 **Track 103**

2 艾琳打電話來說自己要結婚了，請恭喜她。

A: 喂，請問丹尼斯在嗎？

B: 是，我就是。請問您哪位？

A: 我是艾琳。我下個月要結婚了！

B: 妳說真的嗎？恭喜！

A: 謝謝。

B: 我真為妳開心。

A: Hello, is Dennis there?

B: Yes, speaking. Who's calling, please?

A: This is Erin. I'm going to get married next month!

B: _____ Congratulations!

A: _____

B: _____

Track 104

3　鮑伯剛剛失去了哥哥，請打電話安慰他吧。

A: 喂，我是鮑伯。

B: 噢，鮑伯，我是海倫。**我聽說了你那件不幸的事。**

A: 噢，海倫。

B: 很遺憾你哥哥過世了。

A: 謝謝妳的來電。**妳不知道這對我有多大的幫助。**

A: Hello? Bob speaking.

B: Oh, Bob. This is Helen. _____

A: Oh, Helen.

B: I was so sorry that your brother passed away.

A: Thank you for your call. _____

Answers

隨堂測驗 A

1 Congratulations on　　2 I heard　　3 won the lottery / Are you serious?　　4 Congratulations!
5 I'm sorry to hear that

隨堂測驗 B

1 A little bird told me that you got promoted. / I'm calling to congratulate you.
2 Are you serious? / Thank you. / I'm so happy for you.
3 I heard about your misfortune. / You don't know how much it helps me.

訂位、訂房、訂票等

I'd like to reserve a table for two.

〉〉請跟著 Kevin 一起練習用英語完成生活上的各種預約。

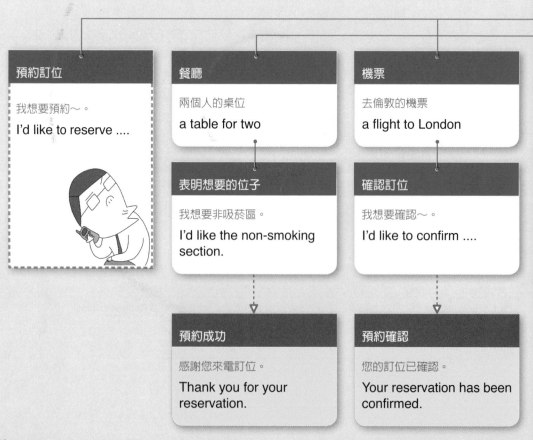

預約訂位

我想要預約～。

I'd like to reserve ....

餐廳

兩個人的桌位

a table for two

機票

去倫敦的機票

a flight to London

表明想要的位子

我想要非吸菸區。

I'd like the non-smoking section.

確認訂位

我想要確認～。

I'd like to confirm ....

預約成功

感謝您來電訂位。

Thank you for your reservation.

預約確認

您的訂位已確認。

Your reservation has been confirmed.

◆ 點菜 **order (v./n.)** 餐廳裡服務生問「準備好點菜了嗎？」就是 Are you ready to order? 或 Can I take your order?。

◆ 預約 **reservation (n.)** 一般用 make a reservation 此片語來表達預約的動作。

◆ 預約～人的桌位 **reserve a table for ...** 注意，餐廳訂「位」不用 seat 這個字，而是要說 table，例如「三個人的桌位」就叫 a table for three。

◆ 確認預約 **confirm the reservation** 在英文裡，要表達「確認」大多是用 confirm 這個字。

◆ 用電話 **by phone** 注意不要說成 by the phone。

◆ 外帶 **takeout (n.)** 另，Is this for here or to go? 即「內用還是外帶？」之意。

◆ 可退款的 **refundable (adj.)** refund 是退錢的意思，字尾 -able 表示「能夠、可以」。

◆ 來回票 **round-trip ticket** 單程票則為 one-way ticket。

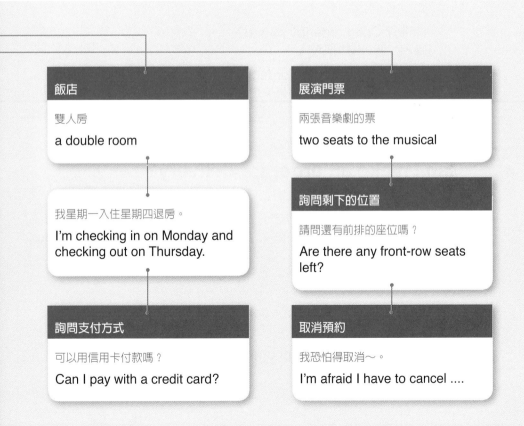

飯店

雙人房

a double room

我星期一入住星期四退房。

I'm checking in on Monday and checking out on Thursday.

詢問支付方式

可以用信用卡付款嗎？

Can I pay with a credit card?

展演門票

兩張音樂劇的票

two seats to the musical

詢問剩下的位置

請問還有前排的座位嗎？

Are there any front-row seats left?

取消預約

我恐怕得取消～。

I'm afraid I have to cancel ....

電話英語通關句 TOP *10*

雖然現今網路訂位非常方便，但偶爾還是無法避免利用電話溝通細節或處理事情。在國外生活或旅遊也同樣有可能遇到必須用英語講電話解決問題的狀況，特別是訂機票、預約飯店與餐廳等。請熟記以下所介紹的句子。

🔊Track 105

Can I order by phone?
我可以用電話點餐嗎？

不論是去餐廳之前先打電話點菜，或是先致電詢問是否可以先點菜稍後直接取餐外帶時都可以這樣問。

A Hello? Can I order by phone?
喂，我可以用電話點餐嗎？

B Sure. We'll take your order, and you can pick it up later.
當然可以。請您先點，待會再來取餐。

Can I make an order for delivery?
我可以點外送嗎？

舉例來說，通常打電話去披薩店的時候，對方會先問 Is this for delivery or pickup [takeout]?（請問您要外送還是外帶？）。在美國因為都要給外送員小費，所以很多人會先打電話去預訂然後自己去拿 [pick up]。

A Can I make an order for delivery, please?
請問可以點外送嗎？

B OK. Can I have your phone number?
好的。請問您的電話幾號？

I'd like to reserve a table for two.

我想訂兩個人的桌位。

打電話去餐廳訂位時就用這個句子。不妨試著在 for 後面加上其他人數練習看看。

A I'd like to reserve a table for four, please.
我想訂四個人的位子。

B Sure. Is this for tonight?
好的。是訂今天晚上嗎？

I need to cancel my reservation.

我必須取消預約。

預約之後如果不得已要取消，打電話去告知是禮貌。特別像是醫院這類的地方，如果做了預約卻沒有出現的話，有些是會罰錢的！另外，如果要變更預約，就說 I need to change my reservation.。

A I have a reservation, but I need to cancel it.
我有預約，但是我必須取消。

B Thank you for calling. Can I have your name, please?
謝謝您來電。請問您的名字是？

Can I pay with a credit card?

可以用信用卡付款嗎？

如果是店家則可以這樣詢問：How would you like to pay?（請問您要如何付款？）。

· Do you accept credit cards?
你們收信用卡嗎？

· Can I charge it to my Visa card?
我可以用 Visa 卡付款嗎？

· I'd like to charge it to my MasterCard.
我想用萬事達卡付款。

Would you like me to put you on the waiting list?

您要不要我幫您排候補？

「候補名單」稱作 waiting list 或 wait list。訂機票時常有機會遇到此情況，雖然已經沒有座位了，但是航空公司為了避免有人取消，仍會接受候補名單。

A Sorry, but we're full Saturday. Would you like me to put you on the waiting list?
抱歉，我們週六已經滿了。您要排候補嗎？

B Thank you. That would be great.
謝謝你。那太好了。

Your reservation has been confirmed.

您的訂位已確認。

訂機票時雖然是「候補」，但是遇到有人取消而變成預約 OK！這時的動詞就是用 confirm。接著在收到訂位號碼 (confirmation number) 並完成付款後就算確保了機位。

A I'm calling you to let you know that your reservation has been confirmed.
我打來通知您的預約已經確認了。

B Thank you. When do I need to pay for the tickets?
謝謝。請問我什麼時候需要付機票錢？

We'd prefer a seat in the non-smoking section.

我們要非吸菸區的座位。

一般餐廳會有非吸菸區 (non-smoking section) 和吸菸區 (smoking section) 的座位之分，訂位時可先指定。

· We'd prefer a table by the window.
我們要靠窗的位子。

· I'd like a private room.
我要訂一間包廂。

· Are there any front-row seats left?
還有前排的座位嗎？

09 Is this ticket refundable?

這張票可以退款嗎？

購買機票時不要因為便宜就下手，要先弄清楚是否可退費、使用上是否有限制 (Are there any restrictions?)，以及改期的話是否須付手續費 (Is there a fee for a schedule change?)。

A Is this ticket refundable?
請問這張票可以退款嗎？

B Yes, it is. But you have to pay a 10% fee.
是的，可以退。不過您必須付一成的手續費。

10 I'd like to reserve a room, please.

麻煩你，我想訂一個房間。

「客房」只要講 room 就好，不需要說 guest room。「請問有空房嗎？」就是 Do you have any rooms available?。

A I'd like to reserve a room, please. I'm checking in on Monday and checking out on Wednesday.
麻煩你，我想訂一間房。我週一入住週三退房。

B OK, let's see .... We have an ocean view room available.
好的，讓我看看……我們有一間海景房是空的。

飯店客房的種類

1. 客房類型

single room　一張單人床的單人房
twin room　兩張單人床的雙人房
double room　一張雙人床的雙人房
king-size bed　一張大雙人床的房間

2. 各種特色的房間

room with a city view　市區景觀的房間
room with a terrace　有陽台的房間
quiet room　安靜的房間
corner room　角落房；邊間房

請確實開口反覆練習，讓自己熟悉這些句型。　**Track 106**

我想～。
I'd like to _____ .

① make a reservation　預約
② reserve a table for three　訂三個人的桌位
③ cancel my reservation　取消我的預約

若是訂機票，可說 I'd like to reserve a seat on the next flight to Tokyo.（我想訂下一班去東京的機位）。

您的預約已～。
Your reservation is _____ .

① confirmed　確認
② canceled　取消
③ all set　完成

取消卻未事先通知，英文叫作 no-show，簡單來說就是沒有出現，而此情況的罰金就叫 no-show penalty。

隨堂測驗 A

請依 CD 所播放的內容，完成下列對話。

🔊 Track 107

試試這樣說～　　　　　　　　　　　　　　　牛刀小試！

1 A: 喂，我有預約，**但是我必須取消。**
B: 好的。請問您預約的是什麼時間？

A: Hello. I have a reservation, _____
_____.

B: OK. When is your reservation for?

2 A: 您好，這裡是喜樂旅遊。您**排了** 1 月 25 號出發的機位**候補**。我打來通知您有機位了，**您的預約已確認。**
B: 噢，真的嗎？謝謝。

A: Hello, this is Joy Travel. You were _____
_____ for a flight on the
25th of January. I'm calling to let you know
that space has opened up, and _____
_____.

B: Oh, really? Thank you.

3 A: 麥可餐廳您好。我能為您服務嗎？
B: 麻煩你，**我要訂明天晚上五個人的桌位。**

A: Michael's Restaurant. Can I help you?
B: Yes, _____
for tomorrow evening, please.

4 A: **我想訂**六月四號起兩個晚上的**房間。**
B: 請問您要怎樣的房間？

A: _____
two nights from June 4th.
B: What type of room would you like?

5 A: 請問您要靠窗還是靠走道的位子？
B: **我要靠窗的位子。**

A: Would you prefer a window seat, or an
aisle seat?
B: _____

請聽 CD 完成下列三組不同情境的對話。

🎵Track 108

1 　請打電話去餐廳訂兩個人的桌位。

A: 大城餐廳您好。我能為您服務嗎？

B: 是的，我想訂今天晚上八點兩個人的位子。

A: 噢，**晚上八點沒有位子了**。但是七點有。

B: 好，那我訂七點。**我們要非吸菸區的座位。**

A: 沒問題。請問您貴姓大名？

A: Hello, Big City Diner. Can I help you?

B: Yes, I'd like to reserve a table for two tonight at eight o'clock.

A: Oh, _____.

　　But we do at seven.

B: OK, then can I reserve one at seven?

_____

A: Sure. Your name, please?

🎵Track 109

2 　請試著訂購表演的門票。

A: 喂，**我想訂兩張**今天晚上表演**的票**。

B: 好的。票價是三十塊美金。請問您要怎麼付款？

A: **可以用信用卡付款嗎？**

B: 當然可以。請問您的卡號是？

A: Hello. _____ for tonight's show.

B: Of course. The price is $30. How would you like to pay?

A: _____

B: Of course. What's your credit card number?

🎵**Track 110**

3   請試著接聽打來預訂飛往洛杉磯的機位的電話。

A: 喂，我想訂十月五日飛洛杉磯的機票。

B: **很抱歉，我們那天沒有機位了。** 您要不要我幫您排候補？

A: 噢……那十月六日呢？

B: **讓我看一下。** 那天有兩班飛往洛杉磯的班機。一班上午十點出發，另外一班下午五點半出發。

A: 下午五點半比較合適我。

B: 好的。能不能告訴我您的英文全名怎麼拼？

A: Hello, I'd like to reserve a flight to L.A. on the 5th of October.

B: _____

   _____

A: Oh ... then how about the 6th of October?

B: _____ We have two flights to L.A. One departs at

   10 a.m., and the other at 5:30 p.m.

A: 5:30 p.m. is better for me.

B: OK. Could you spell your full name in English for me?

Answers

隨堂測驗 A

1 but I need to cancel it   2 on the waiting list / your reservation has been confirmed
3 I'd like to reserve a table for five   4 I'd like to reserve a room for   5 I'd prefer a window seat.

隨堂測驗 B

1 we don't have tables available at eight / We'd prefer a seat in the non-smoking section.
2 I'd like to reserve two tickets / Can I pay with a credit card?
3 I'm sorry, but we are full on that day. / Would you like me to put you on the waiting list? / Let me check.

寒暄問候

I just called to say hi.

〉〉請跟著 Kevin 一起練習用英語和工作夥伴噓寒問暖。

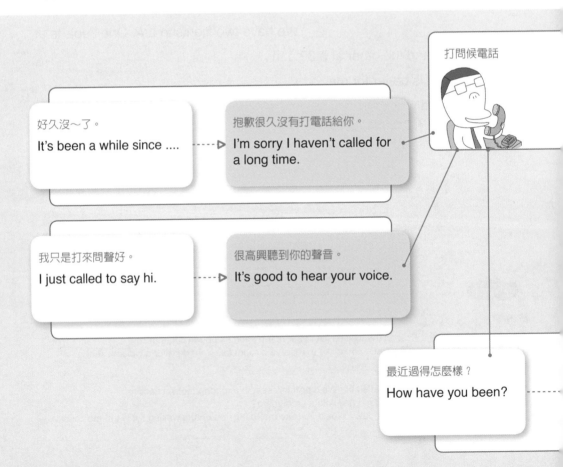

打問候電話

好久沒～了。
It's been a while since ....

抱歉很久沒有打電話給你。
I'm sorry I haven't called for a long time.

我只是打來問聲好。
I just called to say hi.

很高興聽到你的聲音。
It's good to hear your voice.

最近過得怎麼樣？
How have you been?

Kate 老師的重點提示

◆ 打來問好 **call to say hello** 英文沒有類似「問候電話」這樣的用語，所以就說 I just called to say hello/hi.。

◆ 最近過得怎麼樣？ **How have you been?** 也可以說 How've you been doing? / What's up?（很熟的朋友之間使用）。

◆ 謝謝你打電話來 **Thanks for calling.** 電話中聽到對方說出這句話時通常就表示差不多可以掛電話了。

◆ 保持聯繫 **keep in touch** stay in touch 也是同樣的意思。相反地，lose touch with somebody 則為「與～失去聯繫」之意。

◆ 一切如常，沒什麼特別的事 **Business as usual.** 也可以說 Same thing different day.（老樣子）。如果要表達「一樣忙」就說 Busy as usual.。

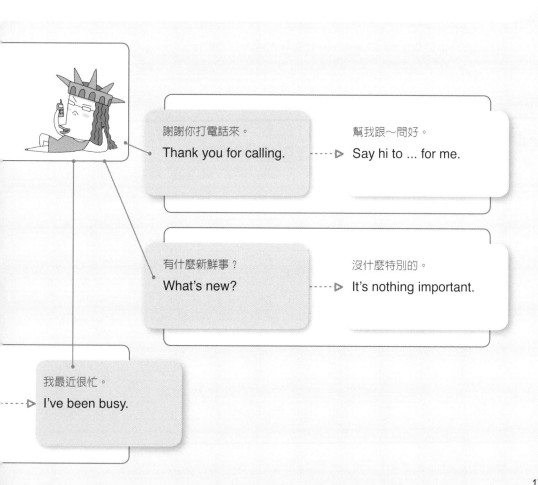

謝謝你打電話來。
Thank you for calling.

幫我跟～問好。
Say hi to ... for me.

有什麼新鮮事？
What's new?

沒什麼特別的。
It's nothing important.

我最近很忙。
I've been busy.

電話英語通關句 TOP 10

我們有時候閒來無事會打電話給朋友互相了解近況。
像這樣沒有特別的事也沒忘記工作夥伴，偶爾打電話
噓寒問暖有助拓展職場上的人際關係。

Hello

🔊 Track 111

I just called to say hi.

我只是打來問聲好。

打電話給許久不見的朋友時可以這樣說，有「打個電話看看你好不好」的感覺。

· I just wanted to hear your voice.
  我只是想聽聽你的聲音。

· I just called to wish you a Merry Christmas.
  我只是打來祝你聖誕快樂。

It's good to hear your voice.

很高興聽到你的聲音。

It's good to ... 指「很高興～」，比方說 It's good to be back home. 是「回到家很開心」的意思。

A I just called to say hello.
   我只是打來問聲好。

B Thank you. It's good to hear your voice.
   謝謝。很高興聽到你的聲音。

It's been a while since I talked to you.

好久沒有跟你說話了。

It's been a while 是「已經很久了」的意思，而 since I talk to you 指「自從我上次跟你講話」。換言之，整句話就是「我好久沒有跟你說話了」之意。It's been a long time since ... 也是類似的表達方式。

A It's been a while since I talked to you!
好久沒打電話給你了！

B Yeah! How have you been?
是啊！你最近過得怎麼樣？

I've been busy.

我最近很忙。

如果想要具體說「忙什麼」，就在 busy 後面加上 with，比方說「我忙著工作」就是 I've been busy with work.。

A I haven't talked to you in a while.
我好久沒跟你講到話了。

B Yes, sorry I haven't called you in a long time. I've been very busy with work.
對啊，抱歉，我很久沒打電話給你。這陣子我一直忙著工作。

What's new?

有什麼新鮮事？

詢問許久沒聯絡的對象有無新消息時就可以說 What's new?。另外，Anything new?、Any good news? 也都很道地。如果沒有什麼特別的近況好說，就回答 Not much. / It's nothing important.。

A How have you been? What's new?
最近如何？有什麼新鮮事？

B Oh, my son is getting married!
噢，我兒子要結婚了！

Week 4 | Sun.1

173

How have you been?

最近過得怎麼樣？

這是在問對方沒有聯絡的那段時間過得如何，將 How are you? 改成了現在完成式。

A It's been so long since I talked to you. How have you been?
好久沒跟你聊天了。最近過得怎麼樣？

B Things have been going well. Busy as always.
情況都還不錯。一直很忙。

Thank you for calling.

謝謝你打電話來。

這句話雖然什麼時候都可以說，但是通常是準備要掛電話的時候會講。另外，用 It was nice talking to you.（很高興跟你通電話）/ It was good to hear your voice.（很高興聽到你的聲音）也 OK。

A It was nice to talk to you. Thanks for calling.
很高興跟你通電話。謝謝你打來。

B You're welcome. I'll talk to you later.
不客氣，下次再聊。

I'm sorry I haven't called for a long time.

抱歉很久沒有打電話給你。

這是很久沒跟對方聯絡時用來向對方表示歉意的說法。

A I'm sorry I haven't called for a long time.
抱歉我很久沒打電話給你。

B That's OK.
沒關係。

Is there anything I can do for you?

有什麼我可以為你做的嗎？

當打電話給身處困難的人時就可以這樣說，相信對方聽到時會感到很窩心。If there's anything I can do for you, let me know. 也是一樣的意思。

A Is there anything I can do for you?
有什麼我可以為你做的嗎？

B No, I'm fine. But it's nice of you to offer. Thanks.
沒什麼事，我很好。不過，謝謝你這樣說。

Say hi to your wife for me.

幫我跟你太太問好。

這個句型很實用，或者也可以說 Tell your wife I said hi.。

A I have to go. Say hi to your wife for me, please.
我得掛了。請幫我跟你太太問好。

B I will. Thanks for calling. Bye.
我會的。謝謝你打來，掰。

🔊**Track 112**

請代我問好

託人代為問候的表達方式隨著親密度的不同而有以下幾種不同的說法。

- Say hi to your boyfriend. 幫我跟妳男朋友問好。
- Give her a hug for me. 幫我給她一個擁抱。
  （在西方，擁抱在熟悉的朋友間是很正常的習慣，通常是女性會這麼說。）
- Give him hugs and kisses. 幫我給他抱抱跟親親。
  （這句話是在用小孩身上的，通常也是女性在說。）

175

請確實開口反覆練習，讓自己熟悉這些句型。　　　🔾**Track 113**

很久沒有～。
It's been a while since _____.

① I talked to you　跟你說話了
② we've had lunch together　和你一起吃午餐了
③ I saw you　看到你了

> 此句型也可以用 It's been a long time since ... 替換，在文法上 since 後面要用過去式，但是口語上也會用現在完成式。

我只是打來～。
I just called to _____.

① say hello/hi　問聲好
② talk a bit　聊聊天
③ give you some good news　告訴你一些好消息

> a bit 是「一點兒」的意思。talk a bit 也可以用 talk for a while 來替換。

OK?

隨堂
測驗 **A**

請依 CD 所播放的內容，完成下列對話。

🔴**Track 114**

試試這樣說～

牛刀小試！

1 A: 喂，我是安娜。
   B: 嗨！**最近過得怎麼樣？**

A: Hello, this is Anna.

B: Hi! _____

2 A: 喂，我是中居。蜜雪兒在嗎？
   B: 噢，嗨！我就是！**好久沒跟你說話了！**

A: Hello, this is Nakai. Is Michelle there?

B: Oh, hi! It's me! _____

_____

3 A: 勞倫斯，很高興聽到你的聲音。
   B: **我也是。有時間再打個電話給我吧。**

A: Lawrence, it's been so good to hear your voice.

B: _____

_____

4 A: 我差不多已經六個月沒有跟你講電話了。
   B: 對啊，**已經好久了。**你最近過得怎麼樣？

A: I think it's been about six months since I talked to you last.

B: Yes, _____.

How have you been?

5 A: 最近過得怎麼樣？
   B: **我一直在忙**一個新案子。

A: How have you been?

B: _____

a new project.

請聽 CD 完成下列三組不同情境的對話。

◉Track 115

1 打電話給久違的珍妮佛吧。

A: 喂，我是湯瑪士霍爾。**珍妮佛在嗎？**
B: 嗨，湯瑪士。我就是。最近過得怎麼樣？
A: 我最近很忙。**抱歉好久沒有打電話給妳。**
B: 沒關係。伊利諾州如何？
A: 非常冷！

A: Hello, this is Thomas Hall. _____

B: Hi, Thomas. This is Jennifer. How have you been?

A: I've been busy. _____

B: That's OK. How's Illinois?

A: Very cold!

◉Track 116

2 打電話給久違的格林小姐問聲好吧。

A: 喂，格林小姐。我是尼可拉斯。好久沒聯絡了。
B: 尼可拉斯？尼可拉斯肯特先生？
A: 是啊！抱歉好久沒打電話給妳。
B: 有什麼新鮮事嗎？
A: **沒什麼。我只是打來問聲好。**
B: 嗯。**你應該多多保持聯絡。**
A: 我知道。我最近有點忙。

A: Hello, Ms. Green. It's Nicholas. It's been a while.

B: Nicholas? Mr. Nicholas Kent?

A: Yeah! I'm sorry that I haven't called for a long time.

B: So what's new?

A: _____ _____

B: Well. _____

A: I know. I've been a little bit busy.

🔊**Track 117**

3   接到許久沒聯絡的艾琳的電話，問問看她的近況吧。

A: 喂，丹尼斯嗎？

B: 我就是。

A: 我是艾琳。好久沒聯絡了，對吧？

B: 對啊。**很高興聽到妳的聲音。**什麼事？

A: 噢，我要搬去馬里蘭了。你就住在附近，對吧？

B: 是啊。妳什麼時候搬來？我等不及跟妳碰面！

A: 我八月會過去。要走前我會再打電話給你。

B: 好極了。**請幫我跟妳先生問聲好。**

A: Hello, Dennis?

B: Speaking.

A: This is Irene. It's been a while, huh?

B: Yes. _____

A: Oh, I'm moving to Maryland. You're near there, right?

B: Yeah. When are you coming? I can't wait to see you!

A: I'll be there in August. I'll call you again before I come out.

B: Great. _____

💬 Answers

隨堂測驗 A

1 How have you been?   2 It's been a while since I talked to you!
3 Same here. / Give me a call when you get a chance.   4 it's been a long time
5 I've been busy with

隨堂測驗 B

1 Is Jennifer there? / I'm sorry that I haven't talked to you in a while.
2 Not much. / I just called to say hello. / You should get in touch more often.
3 It's good to hear your voice. / What's up? / Say hi to your husband, please.

Week

4

緊急求救

This is an emergency.

| 星期日第二堂課 |

>> 請跟著 Kevin 一起練習緊急狀況發生時如何用英語求助。

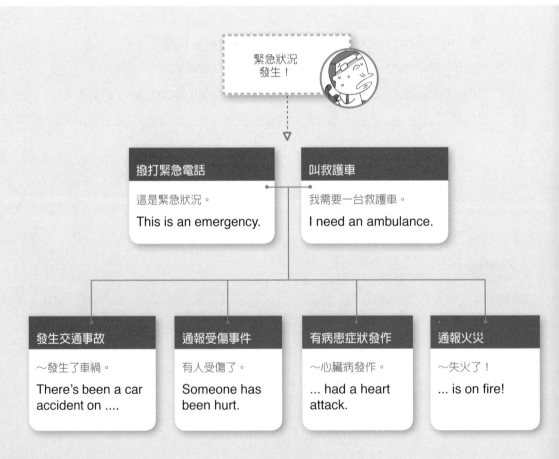

緊急狀況
發生！

撥打緊急電話

這是緊急狀況。

This is an emergency.

叫救護車

我需要一台救護車。

I need an ambulance.

發生交通事故

～發生了車禍。

There's been a car accident on ....

通報受傷事件

有人受傷了。

Someone has been hurt.

有病患症狀發作

～心臟病發作。

... had a heart attack.

通報火災

～失火了！

... is on fire!

Kate 老師的重點提示

◆ 緊急狀況 **emergency (n.)** 急診室就是 emergency room (ER)。

◆ 打 119 **call 911** 在美國旅遊或出差時要注意，美國的緊急電話號碼和我們相反，不要搞錯了！不管是報警、發生火災，或通報醫療緊急狀況都是撥打 911。

◆ 報警 **call the police** 如上所述，在美國報警是打 911，但是「我要報警了！」不能講 I'm going to call 911!，而是要說 I'm going to call the police [cops]!。

◆ 不要掛電話 **Stay on the line.** 打電話去 911 時，接線者為了確認來電者的位置或給予各種資訊，通常會說這句話請對方不要掛斷。有時為了緩解對方的緊張則會說 Stay with me.。

◆ 在途中 **on the way** 告知來電者警察、救護車或消防車已經出動時，就會說 The police are on the way. / The ambulance is on the way.。

◆ 派遣 **dispatch (v.)** 本字和 send 具同樣的意思，而接聽 911 電話的工作人員就叫 dispatcher。

---

911 中心回應

911 緊急服務中心。
911 Emergency Service.

您遇到什麼樣的緊急狀況？
What's the nature of your emergency?

警察已經在路上了。
The police are on their way.

不要掛電話。
Stay on the line.

不要慌張。
Don't panic.

你知道如何做緊急處理嗎？
Do you know first aid?

電話英語通關句 TOP 10

任何人都可能會遇到危急狀況，所以先練好
應對的表達方式吧。同時，也學習一下目擊
火災、犯罪或交通事故時該如何描述。

🔊 Track 118

01 I need an ambulance.

我需要一台救護車。

ambulance 是以母音開始的單字，因此前面的不定冠詞須用 an，而非 a。在美國，救護車
前面的紅字 ambulance 會刻意寫成反的，如此一來，前車的後照鏡上就會倒映出正確的
字樣。

> A My husband is bleeding badly! I need an ambulance right away!
> 我先生流了好多血！我現在馬上需要一台救護車！
>
> B OK. Please stay on the line with me. The ambulance is already on its way.
> 好的，請不要掛電話。救護車已經在路上了。

02 This is an emergency.

這是緊急狀況。

emergency 是「緊急事件、危急狀況」的意思，911 緊急服務中心就是 911 emergency
service，而醫院的急診室則叫 emergency room (ER)。那麼緊急出口呢？答案是 emergency
exit。

> A This is an emergency! Please send an ambulance!
> 這是緊急狀況！請派救護車來！
>
> B Calm down, sir. And tell me where you are.
> 冷靜，先生。告訴我你在哪裡。

What's the nature of your emergency?

您遇到什麼樣的緊急狀況？

美國 911 中心處理的事件包括報警、火災、醫療等各種緊急狀況，因此會詢問通報者這個問題，有時候也會直接問 police, fire, or medical?。nature 一字本身具有「性質、本質」之意，而 nature of emergency 即指「緊急狀況的種類」。

· My house is on fire! 我家失火了！

· Someone has fainted! 有人暈倒了！

· Someone broke into my house! 有人闖進我們家！

The police are on their way.

警察已經在路上了。

台灣雖然有專門受理犯罪相關事件的報警電話，但是在美國無論什麼事都是打 911。注意，police 是集合名詞，動詞要用 are。

A The police are on their way. They'll be there shortly.
警察已經在路上了。他們很快會到。

B Thank you very much! There's a guy outside my window, and I'm just scared because I'm alone in the house.
多謝！我家窗戶外面有一個男人，我一個人在家所以非常害怕。

Stay on the line.

不要掛電話。

在急救隊或警方人員抵達之前為了與通報者保持通話，911 中心會說這句話。Don't hang up. / Stay with me. 也是同樣的意思。

A Stay on the line until the paramedics get there. Where are you injured?
救護人員抵達前不要掛電話。你是哪裡受傷了？

B It's my foot. My foot is killing me!
是我的腳。我的腳快要痛死了！

06 In case of emergency, you can reach me at this number.

萬一有什麼緊急狀況，你打這個電話號碼可以找到我。

in case 是「萬一」的意思；reach 的原意為「到達、達到」，在此則指「與～取得聯繫」。

A In case of emergency, you can reach me at this number.
萬一有什麼緊急狀況，你打這個電話號碼可以找到我。

B OK. I hope I won't have to!
好。希望不會有這個需要！

07 There's been a car accident on West 14th.

西十四街上發生了車禍。

這是車禍報警的表達方式。如果是自己發生了車禍，就說 I've had a car accident.（我發生車禍）。

· Someone got hit by a car.
有人被車撞了。

· There's been a hit-and-run accident on West 14th.
西十四街有人肇事逃逸。

· I hit somebody.
我撞到人了。

· I was rear-ended.
我（的車子）後面被撞到。

08 I ran out of gas.

我的車沒油了。

run out of 就是「～用完了、～沒有了」的意思。I'm out of gas. 同樣也表示車子沒油。

· My car has broken down.
我的車子拋錨了。

· I have a flat tire.
我的車子爆胎了。

09 Leave him alone.

不要動他。

遇到有人受傷時，如果是沒有學過急救的人最好不要隨便觸碰或搬運傷患，等急救人員來處理才是正確的，也就是應該 Wait until the paramedics get there.。

A Is there anything I should do?
有什麼我應該做的嗎？

B No. Just leave him alone. The paramedics are on the way.
沒有，不要動他。急救人員已經在路上了。

10 My son needs to be taken to the hospital.

我兒子需要送醫。

當需要叫救護車去醫院時，就可以利用這個表達方式。

A My son needs to be taken to the hospital. He's fallen and is not moving.
我兒子需要送醫。他摔傷了，現在一動也不動。

B OK, ma'am. Please stay on the line until the ambulance arrives.
好的，女士。請在救護車抵達前不要掛電話。

急救人員

paramedic [ˌpærəˈmɛdɪk] 就是「急救人員」，字首 para- 是「準」的意思，也就是說，雖然不是醫院裡正式的醫師，但是有資格的醫療從業人員。本字原意為「傘兵醫護人員」。

請確實開口反覆練習，讓自己熟悉這些句型。　◎Track 119

我需要～。

I need ████████████████.

① an ambulance　一台救護車
② the police　報警
③ the fire department　找消防隊

以下爲一些 911 中心還可能會給的指示：
Go in a room, and lock the door. 進到房間裡，把門鎖上。
Keep quiet. 保持安靜。
Stay calm, and don't hang up. 保持冷靜，不要掛斷。

～已經在路上了。

████████████████ **on the way.**

① The police are　警察
② A fire truck is　消防車
③ An ambulance is　救護車

很多人以爲 cop(s) 是「警察」較爲低俗的講法，但事實上 cop 乃非正式的口語表達方式，比 policeman/policemen 更常用。

OK?

隨堂測驗 A

請依 CD 所播放的内容，完成下列對話。

🔘 **Track 120**

試試這樣説～　　　　　　　　　　　　　牛刀小試！

1 A: 911 緊急服務中心。**請問您遇到什麼樣的緊急狀況？**

B: **我要報警！**

有人闖進我家，現在在樓下！

A: 911 Emergency Service. _____
_____

B: _____

A man has broken into my house. He's

downstairs!

2 A: 救護車什麼時候會到？

B: 已經**在路上**了，很快就會到。我需要您保持冷靜回答一些問題。首先，請查看一下他有沒有在呼吸。

A: _____

B: It's already _____ and

will be there shortly. I need you to be

calm and answer some questions. First,

please check if he's breathing.

3 A: 華盛頓街上失火了！

請派**消防車來！**

B: 華盛頓街的火災已經有人**通報**了。

謝謝。

A: There's a fire on Washington Street!

Send some _____!

B: The fire on Washington Street has

already been _____. Thank you.

請聽 CD 完成下列三組不同情境的對話。

🔊**Track 121**

1 開車時你目擊車禍發生。請試著打電話給 911。

A: 911 緊急服務中心。請問您遇到什麼樣的緊急狀況？

B: **一號高速公路上發生了車禍。**

A: 好的，警察和救護車已經在路上了。您有受傷嗎？

B: 沒有，我只是路過。**不過有人受傷了。**

A: 好的，**請不要掛電話。**

A: 911 Emergency Service. What's the nature of your emergency?

B: _____

A: OK, The police and an ambulance are already on the way. Are you hurt?

B: No, I was just passing by. _____

A: OK. _____

🔊**Track 122**

2 你需要送太太去醫院。請試著打緊急電話。

A: 喂？**這是緊急狀況！**

B: 先生，請問是什麼問題？

A: **我太太需要送醫。**她的腿好像斷了。

B: 好的。請告訴我您的地址，我們會派救護車過去。

A: Hello? _____

B: What's the problem, sir?

A: _____

I think she broke her leg.

B: OK. Just give me your address, and we'll send an ambulance.

⊘Track 123

3 艾利斯街的百貨公司發生了火災！趕快打電話叫消防車。

A: **失火了！請立刻派消防車過來！**

B: 好的。是哪裡發生火災？

A: 艾利斯街，希爾斯百貨公司。

B: 好的，**消防車已經在路上了**。警察也很快會到。**請不要掛斷**。請問您叫什麼名字？

A: 噢，我叫克莉絲緹娜何。

A: _____ _____

B: OK. Where's the fire?

A: On Iris Street. At Hilll's Department Store.

B: OK. _____ The police will

be there soon, too. _____ What's your name?

A: Oh, I'm Christina Ho.

Answers

隨堂測驗 A

1 What's the nature of your emergency? / I need the police!
2 When's the ambulance going to be here? / on the way   3 fire engines / reported

隨堂測驗 B

1 There's been a car accident on Highway 1. / But someone has been hurt. / Stay on the line, please.
2 This is an emergency! / My wife needs to be taken to the hospital.
3 There's a fire! / Send a fire engine right away! / A fire engine is on the [its] way. / Don't hang up.

A. 請利用括弧內的提示填空以完成句子。 🎧 **Track 124**

1 A: 恭喜你畢業了！(graduation)

B: 謝謝。

A: _____

B: Thank you.

2 A: 我想訂三個人的桌位。(table for three)

B: 好的，請問幾點？

A: _____

B: OK, what time?

3 A: 救護車已經在路上了。請不要掛電話。(on the way / stay on the line)

B: 噢，謝謝！

A: _____

B: Oh, thank you!

4 A: 我聽說你升官了！(I heard / promotion)

B: 啊，對呀。上個星期。

A: _____

B: Ah, yes. Last week.

5 A: 我只是打來問聲好。

B: 很高興聽到你的聲音。(hear / voice)

A: I just called to say hi.

B: _____

B. 請將下列對話中文部分翻譯成英文。

 緊急時

🔊**Track 125**

A: 911 Emergency Service. ① 請問您遇到什麼緊急狀況？

B: My baby fell and hurt his head. He's unconscious!

A: OK, ma'am. Stay on the line. ② 我會派救護車過去。

B: Thank you. I'm so scared! He's only five months old!

A: ③ 冷靜, ma'am. What's your name?

B: Yvette. Is my baby going to be OK?

A: ④ 救護車在路上了。

B: Oh, I think it's here already!

A: OK. Don't hang up, Yvette.

Ans.

① _____ ② _____

③ _____ ④ _____

 祝賀

🔊**Track 126**

A: Hello?

B: Hi, Henry! Happy birthday! It's me, Betty.

A: Oh, Betty. Thanks for the birthday wish. How have you been?

B: ⑤ 我過得很好。You?

A: Me, too. ⑥ 只是工作有點忙。⑦ 謝謝妳記得我的生日。

B: Sure. Why don't I buy you lunch this week? You know, to celebrate your birthday.

A: Cool! Thanks!

B: OK. ⑧ 這週六如何？

Ans.

⑤ _____ ⑥ _____

⑦ _____ ⑧ _____

C. 請和 Kate 老師一起模擬接打電話,做雙向問答練習。

* 本單元錄音內容共有兩遍,第一遍的每一句之間保留了較長的間隔,請利用空檔做跟讀練習;練習完之後,請再聽一遍正常語速的版本。

🔊Track 127

接聽電話

請扮演餐廳的角色,練習接 Kate 的電話。

Restaurant : 史密斯海濱小館您好。

Kate : Hi, I have a reservation, and I was wondering if I could change the time.

Restaurant : 好的。請問您貴姓大名?

Kate : Kim, Kate Kim. The reservation is for five people at 5:30 tonight.

Restaurant : 是的,金小姐。請問您要改訂到幾點?

Kate : Could you change it to 6:30, please?

🔊Track 128

撥打電話

請扮演 Kevin 的角色,試著打電話給 Kate。

Kevin : 喂,凱特嗎?我是建文。

Kate : Kevin? Hey! It's been a while since I talked to you.

Kevin : 我知道。你過得怎麼樣啊?我只是想問聲好。

Kate : I'm doing well. My little brother Sean made the soccer team.

Kevin : 真的嗎?太棒了!也許我可以找個時間去看他踢球?

Kate : Of course! You should. He's a great player. In fact, he has a game this Sunday.

* 全篇對話之中文翻譯請左右兩頁對照參閱。

撥打電話

接下來換你練習打電話給餐廳。

Restaurant	: Hello. Smith's Beach Bistro.
Kate	: 嗨，我已經訂了位，不知道可不可以改時間？
Restaurant	: OK. What's your name?
Kate	: 我姓金，金凱特。我訂了今晚五點半五個人的位子。
Restaurant	: Yes, Ms. Kim. What time would you like to change your reservation to?
Kate	: 可以幫我改到六點半嗎？

接聽電話

再來請練習接 Kate 的電話。

Kate	: Hello. Kevin? This is Kate.
Kevin	: 凱特？嘿！好久沒跟妳講電話了。
Kate	: I know. How are you doing? I just wanted to say hi.
Kevin	: 我很好。我弟弟尚恩被選進足球隊了。
Kate	: Really? That's great! Maybe I can watch him play sometime?
Kevin	: 當然囉！妳是應該來。他踢得很棒。事實上他這週日就有一場比賽。

A

1 Congratulations on your graduation!
2 I'd like to reserve a table for three, please.
3 The ambulance is on the way. Please stay on the line.
4 I heard you got a promotion!
5 It's good to hear your voice.

B

① What's the nature of your emergency?
② I'll send you an ambulance.
③ Calm down
④ The ambulance is on its way.
⑤ I'm doing well.
⑥ Just busy with work.
⑦ Thanks for remembering my birthday.
⑧ How about this Saturday?

翻譯

緊急時
A: 911 緊急服務中心。請問您遇到什麼樣的緊急狀況？
B: 我的寶寶跌倒摔到了頭，現在沒有意識！
A: 好的，太太。請不要掛斷電話，我會派救護車過去。
B: 謝謝。我好害怕！他才五個月大！
A: 太太請冷靜。請問您叫什麼名字？
B: 依薇。我的寶寶會沒事嗎？
A: 救護車已經在路上了。
B: 噢，好像已經到了！
A: 好的。請不要掛電話，依薇。

祝賀
A: 喂？
B: 嗨，亨利！生日快樂！我是貝蒂。
A: 噢，貝蒂，謝謝妳的生日祝福。最近怎麼樣？
B: 我很好。你呢？
A: 我也是。就是忙著工作。謝謝妳記得我的生日。
B: 別客氣。這禮拜請你吃個午飯吧！你知道的，慶祝你生日。
A: 太棒了！謝啦。
B: 好。這週六如何？

國家圖書館出版品預行編目資料

上班族週末充電課：電話英文 / Shin Yena 作；
　朱淯萱譯. -- 初版. -- 臺北市；貝塔，2017.07
　　面；　公分
　ISBN 978-986-94176-3-1（平裝附光碟片）
　1. 商業英文　2. 會話

805.188　　　　　　　　　　　　　　106008449

上班族週末充電課：電話英文

作　　者 / 申藝娜 (Shin Yena)　　　審　　閱 / Quentin Brand
譯　　者 / 朱淯萱　　　　　　　　執行編輯 / 游玉旻

出　　版 / 貝塔出版有限公司
地　　址 / 100 台北市館前路 12 號 11 樓
電　　話 / (02) 2314-2525
傳　　真 / (02) 2312-3535
客服專線 / (02) 2314-3535
客服信箱 / btservice@betamedia.com.tw
郵　　撥 / 19493777 貝塔出版有限公司

總 經 銷 / 時報文化出版企業股份有限公司
地　　址 / 桃園市龜山區萬壽路二段 351 號
電　　話 / (02) 2306-6842

出版日期 / 2017 年 7 月初版一刷
定　　價 / 320 元
海外定價 / 美金 14 元
I S B N / 978-986-94176-3-1

喚醒你的英文語感！

折後釘好，直接寄回即可！

100 台北市中正區館前路12號11樓

 貝塔語言出版 收
Beta Multimedia Publishing

寄件者住址 □ □ □

貝塔語言出版
Beta Multimedia Publishing

讀者服務專線（02）2314-3535　　讀者服務傳真（02）2312-3?

客戶服務信箱　btservice@betamedia.com.tw

www.betamedia.com.tw

謝謝您購買本書！！

貝塔語言擁有最優良之英文學習書籍，為提供您最佳的英語學習資訊，您可填妥此表後寄回（免貼郵票）將可不定期收到本公司最新發行書訊及活動訊息！

姓名：_____　性別：□男 □女　生日：____年____月____日

電話：(公)_____(宅)_____(手機)_____

電子信箱：_____

學歷：□高中職含以下　□專科　□大學　□研究所含以上

職業：□金融　□服務　□傳播　□製造　□資訊　□軍公教　□出版

　　　□自由　□教育　□學生　□其他

職級：□企業負責人　□高階主管　□中階主管　□職員　□專業人士

1. 您購買的書籍是？_____

2. 您從何處得知本產品？(可複選)

　　　□書店 □網路 □書展 □校園活動 □廣告信函 □他人推薦 □新聞報導 □其他

3. 您覺得本產品價格：

　　　□偏高 □合理 □偏低

4. 請問目前您每週花了多少時間學英語？

　　　□ 不到十分鐘 □ 十分鐘以上，但不到半小時 □ 半小時以上，但不到一小時

　　　□ 一小時以上，但不到兩小時 □ 兩個小時以上 □ 不一定

5. 通常在選擇語言學習書時，哪些因素是您會考慮的？

　　　□ 封面 □ 內容、實用性 □ 品牌 □ 媒體、朋友推薦 □ 價格 □ 其他_____

6. 市面上您最需要的語言書種類為？

　　　□ 聽力 □ 閱讀 □ 文法 □ 口說 □ 寫作 □ 其他_____

7. 通常您會透過何種方式選購語言學習書籍？

　　　□ 書店門市 □ 網路書店 □ 郵購 □ 直接找出版社 □ 學校或公司團購

　　　□ 其他_____

8. 給我們的建議：_____

_____

喚醒你的英文語感！

Get a Feel for English !